A Woman's World
and the
Men In-Between

MG WANJIKU

TABLE OF CONTENTS

DEDICATION

To the women and men who work hard to protect others in their adversities. And in memory of my mother, who succumbed to horrific violence, and for my deceased loving, humble father.

PREFACE

Born Free

It doesn't have to end this way.
It could be your grandmother, your mother, your aunt, your daughter or your granddaughter.

In the human race, we have a male and a female child. They are supposed to be born free and equal – not in the matter of biology or physical strength, but by the factors that define them as human beings.

However, many young girls and women have their feathers plucked before they can learn how to fly, rendering them powerless and hopeless. Ladies dignity and self-worth are stripped away. They are kept helpless by obstacles imposed on them by their culture, the men around them, and their women agents.

With any attempt they make to take baby steps and push them forward, they are pulled down and toppled over by those in power to silence them. They are tormented and left without a voice and the strength to fight back.

To some, servitude is for life. Women who manage to detangle themselves from the cultural yoke are possibly unaware of what lies on the horizon in an uncertain venture. They embark on the secret voyage of their lifetime, ready to tackle whatever is ahead of them. In spite of this, the female's determination to break free doesn't come without risks, and the authorities do little to rescue them. Their gender becomes a curse and makes it harder for them to know where to turn. And at times, they may be left dishevelled in mind and soul.

Some might dwell in their situation for a lifetime, as they may not know whether breaking free is better or worse. Others might let hope and their willpower slip away and invite defeat, as they never see themselves being whole again.

If only a curious eye could spot their calamity and despair and provide them with help and support, they might make a change in their circumstances. Unique challenges and concerns need specific guidance and support for survival.

A woman's spirit never dies. It is hidden within, waiting to be rescued and to fight on. Then again, many females scan in all directions, searching 360 degrees with pondering eyes filled with sadness and despair, wishing and hoping that someone would notice their plight and save them from their distress. However, for most of them, their wish and hope keep on burning until their journey to liberation comes to a tragic end.

CHAPTER 1

A Woman's Journey

Many women's lives are like most extended expedition full of obstacles, with some
sweetness and some bitterness along the way as they seek for their queendom.
They live with hope, determination, and the desire to overcome the barriers that
subject them to remaining in their cocoons and obstruct
them from becoming the butterflies they want to be. This desire is what inspires
many of them to fight on for justice, look into the horizon, and strive to conquer
the limitations that prohibit them
from progressing in life. Their wish is to get to the other side of the hurdles to
their free world and raise their hands up in the air and shout, "We have
done it!"

A woman is born free to be a ruler of her destiny. But her journey of self-discovery, acceptance, and the desire for independence never ends. From the time a girl says hello to the world with a cry at birth, her birth signifies an addition to the most robust yet downgraded group of human beings on earth and the beginning of hardship and prosperity if only luck prevails.

Intelligence and hard work, in some cases, become insignificance, as a female's progress may depend on inner strength, fate and the people around her. The lack of choice is something she shares with other girls worldwide. She may have no say in what happens in her life, as certain cultures expect a woman to accept confinement in the home and adhere to the community norms and societal stigmas that paint girls and women as a weaker gender without question.

The extent of misery is defined by family members, the community, the society, the men, the law, and her ability (or inability) to break free. Women and young girls may have the strength within them to know what they want or to choose their destiny, but their rights are taken away by those in power. The social order swiftly slides in and squeezes the life from matters of the heart, turning them into a resource or possession and leaving their queendom in ruins.

For that reason, their liberty is restricted, and they are conditioned to their situation. Moreover, gender plays a significant role in how women are viewed by society, and they are never safe.

One young girl wasn't ready to conform to societal beliefs about women's inferiority and customary norms.

She knew that she was capable of making her own choices at a young age. It was as if she was born with a vision of rescuing women from the yoke that had been placed on them by men's power and the control that brainwashed women's minds in her village in savannah land in Kenya.

Removing blindfolds from women's eyes, the tape that covered their mouths, and the chains that bound their hands and feet were what she strived to achieve. She believed she could inspire the women to have a voice and look at themselves and say in unison, "We are somebody, and we can do it. Together we can conquer oppression, discrimination, and inequality of opportunities and have the same rights as men!" She felt failing to take her first step to freedom would have been like admitting defeat.

To save herself from the barbaric practices towards girls in her community, she settled for a journey, without contemplating or looking back, lest she got stuck in the culture. With head held up high, she walked majestically like a cat out of a basket towards her future, without a care in the world. She moved through the jungle, not knowing where her next home was going to be.

Her strength, commitment, and determination to emancipate herself and to be a motivation to other girls and women were undeniable. It was the first time she had a total charge of her destiny, and she felt lucky to be alive.

However, her journey was not a walk in the park. She paid a high price for her failure to keep her mouth shut. What compelled her to raise her head up high in stormy waves behind closed doors were her willpower, her strength of mind, and her belief in herself that she could do it.

She realised she was her own person, and no other human being could have power over her. She believed equality of opportunities and justice for all individuals is paramount. She thought a person's effort, persistence, determination, strength, and support should determine the possibilities layout before him or her and that these characteristics, not the dictates of other people, should define what a person may become.

She convinced herself she could be and do what her heart desired. As a result, she was sure she was a warrior princess. After all, she had to rely on her ability to fight for her rights because, if she didn't, no one would. She convinced herself that she could conquer her world. But with her confidence suppressed along the way, she endured a ferocious draining battle for survival. Her only strengths left were her brain and beauty.

She was left helpless without a vision ahead of her. She wondered whether her courage and the purpose for which she was fighting for would sail her through. She was ready to breathe the fresh air in her free world. But her liberty was short-lived, as it depended on one single person.

Therefore, gaining her independence was a matter of life and death.

3

CHAPTER 2

The Birth of a Princess

Time for joy.

Near the Maasai Mara plains, with its vibrant wild animals trotting about, lay a Maasai village. The smoke pierced through the door of a manyatta (a Maasai hut made of sticks, grass, cowhide, and cow dung) and curled up into the sky.

The manyatta had had a facelift the previous day, and the walls were smeared with fresh warm moist cow dung to seal the cracks on the walls. Its lingering smell, like a strong perfume, was still in the air. The shelter had no windows, and it was filled with smoke. The fumes from the fire escaped from the room through the forgotten cracks and into the open air. As it curled up into the sky, it was greeted by the rising yellow morning sun in the bright blue sky.

In the hut, Linnet, a twelve-year-old girl with a clean-shaven head, colourful beaded jewellery draped around her neck, and earrings dangling from her earlobes had just lit the fire. In the settlement, women do all the tough jobs, such as building work, fetching firewood, milking the cows, carrying the water, taking care of the family, and household chores while the men rest in the shade as they watch the women at work.

Any outsider entering the home could have easily mistaken Linnet for a child, but she was somebody's wife and heavily pregnant. Her huge stomach seemed to weigh her down because of her small frame.

She appeared to be lost in thoughts as she paced up and down in the hut, biting her lower lip with her forehead creased as she held her humongous belly and stroked it vigorously. It was not the usual fluttering of what was growing inside her that bothered her but a different feeling that she had experienced throughout the night, and it had intensified. She was afraid of revealing any sign of distress to her husband Leboo, a fifty-year-old man, for fear of being beaten or ridiculed for demonstrating weakness.

Right through her pregnancy, she was advised by her co-wives who were in their twenties and thirty years old to abstain from drinking milk to avoid fattening her unborn baby. She was told having a chunky baby would make giving birth complicated. Therefore, she refrained from drinking milk, thinking the delivery would be as easy as playing a pretend game with a doll.

She persevered with the pain, thinking it would go away and put it down to a severe stomach ache because she did not want to complain about it. However, the agony became unbearable. She felt as if her intestines were being cut into pieces inside her stomach. She thought of calling her husband back into the house, but the thought of it made her shake like a leaf. He had warned her never to speak to him soon after he woke up, until after he had his tea.

On that bright morning, the dew shone like pieces of glass on the grass, as the cows and goats had not stepped on it. The animals were still in their shed, and the cows mooed while the goats bleated as they eagerly waited to be let out of the shed to graze on the green pasture when it was still moist and juicy.

Leboo had gone outside to tend to the animals while Linnet lit the fire to make tea. As she bent down to add firewood to the three-stoned stove on the floor, the discomfort in her belly intensified. As she paced around the room anxiously, and placed the pot of water on the flaming fire, to make breakfast for her husband was the last thing on her mind.

Beads of sweat rolled down her forehead, and in a soft voice, she said to herself, "Be brave. Be brave." Nevertheless, the thrusting in her stomach built up, and it became stronger and stronger. Suddenly, she grabbed a blanket from the wooden bed, covered her mouth with it, and screamed loudly without attracting the attention of her partner and her in-laws. She strode around the room, hoping the aching would cease before Leboo came back into the manyatta.

She was frightened that she hadn't made tea. And consequences would follow if she lazed around. She knew she could not bear Leboo's beating in addition to the agony she was experiencing. She tried to do her duties as a wife, but her body seemed to let her down.

Before long, a gush of water rushed down between her legs, and as she stared at the puddle beneath her feet, she prayed that her husband wouldn't humiliate or chastise her for urinating on the floor. She considered him a master of discipline, and she obeyed his rules. In spite of this, he accused her of being childish and not behaving like a grown woman. He had to give her instructions on what to do in everything. At the time, Linnet had been married for two years, yet she struggled to be the sort of woman her husband wanted her to be.

Despite the knowledge that the life she led wasn't what she had anticipated, she could not return to her parents' house. Her fate was sealed the day her parents accepted the dowry from her husband when she was ten years old. She was now his property, and he had the right to her life and absolute power over her. At that point, she knew she had no choice when it came to her future.

She recalled that, after undergoing through 'female circumcision' a rite of passage from childhood into womanhood at the age of ten, she was finally considered a woman ready for marriage. She had been forced to terminate her studies and step into the role of a woman. Leboo had booked her for a wedding when she was eight years old, and he had increasingly become impatient – tired of waiting to take her home as a wife. Her parents didn't want to give her away straight away despite the fact he had threatened to seek another young wife if the marriage couldn't take place soon. As a result, her parents planned to have her undergo the traditional rite of passage; Leboo couldn't receive her uncircumcised, and they didn't want to lose the dowry.

Therefore, after the 'cutting' before she'd recuperated, the women herded her like a cow to the abattoir in Leboo's hands while she was still raw from her ordeal. "You have become a woman, and therefore you have to leave your parents' house and set your own," they said.

Linnet didn't comprehend what it meant to have her own home or a husband. She screamed and refused to have a house or a spouse and told them she was only a child and wanted to go to school. She wailed and begged the women to save her, but her screams were drowned by the women covering her mouth with their dirty, greasy hands as they laughed. She pleaded with them not to abandon her, but her pleas fell on deaf ears. The more she demanded to be set free, the more they dragged her towards her new shelter. The women told her she had no choice. They had gone through a similar custom. She was not special.

To keep the women from pulling her, she sat on the ground, grabbed the plants on the ground, and held them tightly in her hands. However, she was outnumbered, and the women lifted her up like a feather. She bit the women's hands, but they beat and dragged her into Leboo's hands as if she was a piece of meat. They left her for him to devour her like a hungry hyena. The females laughed and danced as she screamed in the den while her new husband grinned and thanked the women for bringing her to the hut.

Her first night with her spouse was like being thrown into a furnace. She shrieked in anguish as her husband tossed her like a rag doll as she performed the conjugal duties of a wife. She had thought that her husband would have pity on her, but instead, he aggressively pinned her to the floor, slapped her and ordered her to keep quiet whenever she begged for mercy.

Despite trying to be a good wife, she could not bear the weight of his sweaty body on top of her and the excruciating pain in her thin frame. But she had nowhere to run. With escape routes blocked, and the women in her village ready in waiting to capture her and force her back if she escaped, she had no other option other than to persevere with her anguish, hoping it would end soon.

To make the issue worse, no matter how many times she had wished to perish, she had survived to face another day.

As Leboo tended to the animals, Linnet paddled in a flood of water gushing down between her legs. The water seemed like a waterfall streaming from her body. She wondered why there was such a surge of liquid, as this had never happened before. As the water ceased, the pain increased.

Then it went away for a few minutes before it gathered its strength and struck again. That's when Linnet realised something was not quite right.

She shouted for her in-laws who lived in the boma (an enclosure protecting the family homestead) before remembering she had been instructed by her co-wives that, as a woman, she had to be resilient and avoid displeasing her husband to appease his temper. He had an intense look that scared her, and nothing she did was ever good enough. In spite of this, she couldn't take the pain any longer.

As Leboo was about to let the animals out of the shed, he heard shouts from the hut. He quickly shut the gate and turned to attend to his wife's wailing.

He sped back to the manyatta. On the way, he met his wives dashing from the homestead speeding towards his hut and followed them. The family found Linnet on the dusty floor near the fireplace, heaving and writhing in anguish, drenched in sweat, with part of the blanket clenched in her teeth. She told the women her intestines were being ripped into pieces with a blunt sword. One glance at her and the women knew it was time.

One of the ladies rushed to alert the local traditional midwife of the impending birth. Leboo was instructed to leave the shelter while the women prepared a cowhide on the floor, ready to welcome the new addition to the family. Leboo remained calm, and he went back to tend to the animals. It was not the first time his young brides had given birth. He had four wives who he had married as children, so he wasn't worried about Linnet giving birth.

In the hut, when the labour pain deepened, Linnet couldn't stop herself from shouting. The women told her to stop screaming because she was now proving she was a real woman by giving birth. What was happening to her was something that happens to women when in labour, they told her. Linnet couldn't understand how any woman could persevere such horrifying anguish for hours and not say a word. With all the pushing, her legs were like noodles. She felt as if she had poured out all her energy, and she was already nearly out of breath when a woman's voice shouted, "Push. Push. Puuuush!"

She breathed in, and with one mighty thrust, she pushed as hard as she could as the midwife shouted, "I can see some hair. Push!" But she was unable to continue advancing. She had used all her energy, and her tiny frame could take it no more. She was drenched in sweat, and a woman fanned her with a piece of cowhide.

The midwife grew frantic. She didn't know what to do next and with the unsterilised blade in her hand, she cut Linnet's birth canal as Linnet slowly regained some strength and pushed, shouting, "I am dying!"

To save the mother and baby from death, a healthy baby girl was forcefully pulled out of her womb and into the world screaming, followed by her twin brother, who was named Lemayian (meaning he was the blessed one). The baby girl was given the name Jenny Naeku (Naeku meaning she was born early in the morning).

Linnet considered Jenny's sudden cry significant; it demonstrated that she had arrived, and she wanted to be noticed. The exclamation was powerful, a different kind from those heard throughout the homestead. The women said there is no place in the village for big-mouthed girls like Jenny. Furthermore, her right fist was clenched and raised up in the air as she screamed.

However, despite her cries, there were no tears in Jenny's eyes. It seemed like the newborn was desperate for something as she glared straight ahead and appeared to notice the people around her. The women commented that Jenny was going to be a strong-willed child.

It is against the norm in the community for a girl to be powerful and dominant.

From the safety of her mother's womb, Jenny had no idea of her destiny. However, her mother hoped things would be different for her, and wished her daughter wouldn't go through similar suffering she had endured.

There was no worry about Jenny's twin brother, as Linnet believed he had a place in the community and in the society. He, unlike Jenny, would have been valued and treasured by his father.

As she thought about her young stolen life, the new mother hoped that Jenny would have an education and break the cycle of discrimination against women. She desired to protect her infants as she cuddled them in her arms, but Linnet had no idea what she was expected to do with the babies. Her small arms couldn't hold the two newborns together. She relied on the women to guide her on what to do, but the baby boy did not survive the birth ordeal and died soon after birth.

Her joy of giving birth combined with mourning for her dead son and health concerns took a different turn. Her birth canal had been torn like a piece of cloth, thus causing a fistula. She was unaware it was the start of her misery, as urine trickled down her feet uncontrollably. She sought out advice from the women for her ailment, and she was told her body would rectify itself – that the condition would get better with time. But it got worse. Everyone covered their noses whenever she was amongst other people because of the stench that she produced, as she grew desperate for a solution.

Sanitary towels were something Linnet had never seen. She had to tear pieces of her clothes and wear them as sanitary pads, which meant she ensured they were continually washed. Her husband, on the other hand, viewed her as a curse and someone who had brought shame to the family. He used and abused her as a woman of no value because she had failed to carry another pregnancy.

Leboo expected to get wealthy through his daughter's dowry payments. Nevertheless, he also longed for Linnet to have a son. And if she couldn't perform the duty of producing an heir, in his eyes, she had no value in the home, and he planned to marry another young wife.

Despite everything, Linnet persevered with the abuse and humiliation from her husband and her co-wives, who were mature women. Linnet didn't understand what was happening, but she was aware the only way to gain recognition by her man was to have a male child. She prayed day and night for it to happen so that she could obtain respect from him, but she kept on miscarrying the pregnancies.

She lived with the humiliation and vowed not to speak about her difficulties to avoid psychological torture. She couldn't leave her husband because it would have brought dishonour to her family, her spouse, and her parents may have been forced to return the dowry to her husband. Furthermore, there was no guarantee she could remarry because of her condition and stigma. After all, news had spread in the community that she leaked like a tap, and she was afraid no man would accept her, with the infirmity and a child to look after.

She sensed that leaving Jenny with Leboo would mean her daughter would be more than likely to fall into a fate similar to her own. Jenny would, no doubt, undergo circumcision and ultimately married off to a senior man with livestock. She knew that, even if she was lucky enough to get another partner, Jenny might well be rejected by the new in-laws because of the stigma of bringing another man's child into the

11

homestead. She was also concerned she may be forced by the in-laws to give Jenny up for marriage at an early age to get rid of her.

Linnet had observed the women, and young girls in her village suffer in silence. They felt they had no say and no way out of their situations. They were surrounded by people who suppressed them when they rebelled or complained of mistreatment. Therefore, they did what the men wanted them to.

She had witnessed families who had gone through trauma, and she did not want her daughter to suffer. She knew her life was not perfect, but it was not different from most women in the village. They are slaves of their culture, and when life becomes unbearable, there is nowhere to run.

Linnet knew she had no power to make choices regarding the future of their daughter. Leboo made the decisions on what went on in the home, and from the moment she gave birth to Jenny, she knew her destiny was sealed. Jenny's life's course was drawn, and her future was mapped before she could make little baby steps or say her first word.

She was her father's property and therefore, could be sold off for a few cows and goats to the highest bidder. Cattle determines a man's wealth and a source of food in the form of meat, milk, and blood to drink; Plus, cowhide is used for beddings, clothing, and house restoration. Age and love have nothing to do with the customary marriage. In the village, a girl's value is considered to be marriage, home keeping, and childbearing. Thus, her rights and choices are taken away before knowing she has any.

Linnet wanted better things for Jenny. She craved to ensure that her daughter could pursue a different path, even though she knew doing so would risk her life if she disobeyed her husband's intentions concerning their daughter.

CHAPTER 3

The Women of the World

It does not matter what part of the globe a woman comes from. Her experiences are likely to be similar if her fate is in the hands of a man.

Jenny was interested in learning about girls' lives from a young age. She listened to the stories her mother told her about girls and sort for information from newspapers. She went to school as a child and had learned to read quickly. Her curiosity led her to discover that being a woman is insignificant in her community and around the globe.

She discovered that men are in charge, not only in her village but around the world. Men pull women like an elastic band until they break and only punished by a slap on the back of their hands by the communities and the authorities. The men know they have louder voices than females. Linnet said to Jenny, "my daughter, it's time women rise up and protect their own without fear, or forever we shall remain silent. A girl's age is never a concern when a male suitor is available. Negotiations about the girl's worth commence, and bride price discussion begins."

Jenny had noticed when she read the newspapers, girls in some countries have to pay a groom price to be married. Therefore, having too many girls in a family is like a curse. The girls are considered a burden if their families have little money or when a male suitor is not secured. On the other hand, in Jenny's community, the men pay the bride price.

Jenny saw the plight of girls worldwide through her village life. Marriage agreement between the families of the girl and the man means that the deal is sealed. A girl is not allowed to break the transaction, regardless of her circumstances or marital woes, as she becomes her husband's property after marriage. She has no choice, no ability to think about or pursue what she wants. She has to face her spousal duties and avoid shaming and dishonouring the family by running away or by choosing a partner without family involvement. Disobedience and not following the traditions mean death for the girls.

She understood a land title deed come with conditions of use, but with a woman, a man is entitled to use her; however, he wishes. She realised that many women live in vulnerable situations despite making little steps in liberating themselves from men's shackles.

They experience physical, emotional, social, and financial violence; mistreatment; and rape; and they are forced to submit to their partner's demands and control without a complaint.

Many of them own nothing in the household. Women become part of their husband's commodities, and they are last in the hierarchy in the home. The cows and goats have more value than women. Jenny noticed that, during feasts, the women and girls were only allowed to eat leftover meat or cows and goats' intestines and stomachs. The juicy mouth-watering roasted steak meat was consumed by the men and boys under the watchful eyes of the women and girls.

Her mother told her that being a victim of rape, especially by white foreigners, was enough for a woman to be shunned by the community. She would be considered contaminated and likely to bring bad luck to the community. A child born out of the encounter had to be murdered.

Tradition dictates women's status in the community, and the husbands become the morality police. It doesn't matter where a woman runs to; indeed, the man catches up with her. Furthermore, he has full support and permission from the family, community, and society to treat a female how he wants with little or no repercussion.

Hurting women make men who mistreat females' macho men in their own eyes. But are they?

Jenny considers such men cowards for attacking their partners and wives. Even though she had strong views against the mistreatment of girls and women, she was raised to view a male child as superior to her. It became evident to her as she grew up that she might never taste the flavour of having a choice in her life or determine her position in society. Education was not a guarantee that her life would be peaceful either. She saw many girls' studies terminated by their parents so they could offer them for marriage at a young age and acquire cows, goats, and some sugar.

Besides, she sensed panic in some woman's eyes whenever their husbands' names were mentioned. It seemed many things made these women stay in their abusive relationships, including threats and fear; children; hardship; and being brainwashed into believing they were not useful, attractive, or good enough to find someone else to love them. Shame and stigma reinforced by the culture of blaming women for not working hard to save their marriages, compelled them to stay.

15

Keeping quiet about family violence was crucial to protect the family's dignity and honour. Jenny came to understand that domestic violence had no bounds. It cut across all cultures, race, educational levels, and generations. Women are not safe, regardless of their status or position in life.

Equipped with the knowledge she had gathered about women and suffering, Jenny decided to be recognised as equal to men in society.

She vowed never to settle for the weaker sex tag. Jenny knew that a princess, with all the gold, glitter, and the silver spoon that came with the title, there lay within a tormented soul – a princess with her mouth tightly shut. She was pretty sure that a man stands in between a woman in her world.

Jenny determined there was no way her efforts would be hindered by the men that surrounded her or by the women who believed that women belonged to the homestead, childbearing, domestic chores, and pleasing men. She wanted to be different and to be accorded similar respect as men. She was eager to learn why men dominate the world. She was sure the men's dominance had nothing to do with the power of their physique but by the force of mind and control.

From a young age, Jenny was aware that being passive and submissive to a man is key to keeping peace at home.

But she categorically disagreed with the notion. Jenny didn't believe men were superior to her or that she should sit on the fence when she was wronged. She felt the women in her village did whatever they could to please their men and paid no attention to their personal progress in life. They worshipped their men as gods – not because they thought they were magnificent, but out of fear.

Jenny was head high from the moment she hit her teenage years. She wanted to involve herself in everything and do what boys did. For example, looking after animals instead of just cooking and cleaning.

She also wanted to get involved in doing different things so that she could empower other girls and demonstrate to them they can do anything they set their minds on. She was a character that was unheard of in the community. Girls had their place in society, and that was where they belonged, but Jenny thought otherwise.

She wasn't ready to be answerable to a man's demands. She wanted to be part and parcel of the governance in the village and expected to participate and be included in decision-making in the family and the community matters.

She felt she should never be sidelined because of her gender, as she had the capability and the capacity to contribute to the community development. She aspired for recognition as a modern girl of the twenty-first century – an independent woman who could make decisions that were beneficial to the mutual concerns within the family and the community and who could take care of herself.

She had a vision and longed for women to reject humiliation in relationships and degrading treatment of girls, such as virginity testing before marriage, widow inheritance, and fight for emancipation from the chains of male dominance.

She recognised women's weaknesses consist of fear, lack of unity, competition and cold war with each other. This makes it difficult for them to protect young girls from defilement within the community. She wanted to stop the trend of destruction, but it was a battle she could not fight alone.

As much as she hoped to make some changes, she knew she had to overcome challenges. Those in authority are mainly male, and she knew they are unlikely to take the matter seriously. She also thought some women collaborate with the men and fail to fight for the girls' rights because it is a practice that has been handed to them throughout generations and they are not ready to abandon it.

She opposed the belief that she was incapable of being her own boss. She felt that the men should bow at her feet if she were going to do the same for them, and she vowed that none of it – not a religion, tribal customs, power, or control – was going to change her or her aspirations in life. At the back of her mind, she had a vision that troubled her, and she wanted to make it a reality in adulthood.

She observed that women were willing to resolve family issues, but they demonstrated no joy behind closed doors; the village turned into a battlefield, where only the women were casualties. They were violently beaten and kicked around by their men in every corner in the community. But then again in public, they smiled and continued with their daily chores as if nothing had happened.

Jenny was aware that, in every corner of the globe, there are battlefields where women and girls are the victims. Moreover, whenever the females seek help from the elders, they are blamed for not treating their husbands with respect and for not being submissive wives.

Additionally, parents refuse to allow their daughters to come back home after the breakdown of a marriage; such girls are considered a burden to the family, and they are encouraged to stay with their spouses to avoid the girl's parents returning the dowry to the man. Therefore, the girls are encouraged and forced to humble themselves and seek forgiveness from their husbands, despite being the victims.

They mask the pain in their hearts and grow a thick skin to survive. Their culture obstructs them from fighting for their liberty. Jenny thought it is odd that some women feel it is the norm to experience the abuse and consider it a sign of love from their partners and a way of correcting their mistakes.

She realised they are socialised at a young age to believe a man takes control of the homestead, and that was what her parents moulded her to accept. The women knew their place and avoided retaliation. Jenny saw some of the women curled up in a corner sobbing quietly to avoid being heard by the neighbours. Whenever she looked at the ladies, she knew they were in a battle that they could not fight on their own – without collaboration between females and empowering each other to say enough is enough.

She reckoned the females in authority humiliate womenfolk because they are governed and ruled by the male and work according to men's orders and standards. Such women are used as secret weapons by the men, forced to fight their fellow females while the men watch the women's queendoms fall apart. The women traitors call it the duty of service. Their choice contributes to the vicious cycle of women suffering.

The absence of harmony among womankind makes their power ineffective in their fight for recognition, dignified treatment, and equal rights.

Jenny thought that, if the women gathered together, executed their agenda on how to deal with the issues affecting them, and never back down until they get what they deserve, they would win their struggles.

However, she recognised that, although even as a group, they have a voice, oppression push them to a state of submission and silence. Women are made to feel their existence has no value. They view the community and their homes as their safety net, but at the same time, they are isolated and forced to conform to societal pressures. Furthermore, their naivety and helplessness contribute to their persecution.

Jenny knew she was destined to endure a similar destiny as her mother had. Therefore, making a tough decision before her childhood was stolen was crucial. She knew that wrangling loose from her cultural traditions was not an easy task. She decided that, if she was to be with a man, it had to be her heart's desire and choice. She considered the matter of the heart as a private matter, and no one should impose it on another person.

CHAPTER 4

The Family's Top Secret

Behind closed doors is where it happens.

Jenny's mother sheltered her and hoped she would be independent and be the one to break the cycle of oppression among women in the village. Then again, she could not tell her daughter of her hopes, for fear of her husband's brutality if he knew she was encouraging Jenny to disobey their tradition.

Right from the day of Jenny's birth, Linnet had faith her little girl would figure things out for herself and stand firm for her rights and the rights of other girls. She visualised her daughter being a free spirit and striving to be released and fly like a butterfly without restriction. Hence, she knew for Jenny to achieve her goal, she had to support her decisions in secrecy. She also knew that Jenny had to have the strength of a woman to fight her battle, as she believed it was never going to be easy for her.

Jenny was aware of the opposition she was likely to encounter ahead of her. She knew that, while the women remain divided on the matter of safeguarding themselves and their daughters, there is no way the battle of male domination and violence against women will ever be won. She recognised liberation for females is a job that requires precision and unity among women.

Linnet's painful experience made her wish for Jenny to have the courage to pluck a new leaf and sail through to a new life. She sheltered her from the piercing eyes of the men in the village from birth. Jenny was a beautiful child, and her mother was afraid she would be booked for marriage instantly.

Linnet didn't want the history of what had happened to her to be repeated. She felt her daughter had a whole life ahead of her. She wanted Jenny to have an education and become a lawyer, a leader, or whatever she wanted to be. She wanted her to be an independent woman and to fight for women's rights, but she had no say in her daughter's destiny. Jenny's father made all the decisions, and her mother's mouth was sealed, and she couldn't oppose his verdict.

Therefore, Linnet pretended to persuade Jenny to go through circumcision in her father's presence. However, in his absence, she encouraged her to resist. She wished the practice could be abolished and those performing it and promoting it locked up for subjecting the young girls to unnecessary torture. She hoped that Jenny's father would change his mind and see that Jenny was likely to have a better future if they educated her, rather than give her up for marriage to gain a few cows and goats.

As Jenny slept, she heard whispers in the darkness. She slowly rolled over in her cowhide bed near the fireplace as she listened to her name being mentioned.

In spite of her mother's support of her resistance of the cultural customs, Jenny overheard a conversation, which made her muscles tense as her heart beat loudly "boom, boom!" Her parents spoke in low tones, thinking she was fast asleep. She gently crept to the edge of her bed so that she could hear what her parents were discussing. Listening to them was painful. Her bed was only separated from her parents' bed by a wall made of sticks and cow dung. She heard her father say she was becoming too old for marriage, and it was time for her to undergo the rite of passage in preparation to be given away. She listened attentively and refused to leave her life to chances.

It was her mother's week to accommodate her father in their manyatta. His wives had a schedule that told them when they were to house him. But it seemed he regularly spent nights in her mother's manyatta, trying to convince her mother about something. Jenny had warned her parents never to subject her to tribal customs.

She got out of the bed and peered through the gaps on the wall. It was dark inside the room, but the bright light from the moon penetrated through the cracks on the roof of the manyatta and shone directly on her mother's face. She saw her mother's face looking down, her cheeks resting on her palms as Jenny's father continued telling her that they had to set a date for Jenny's rite of passage.

Her father didn't like the fact that Jenny was stubborn, and at the age of fourteen, he wanted her married fast. Jenny heard her father mention there was a man in the neighbouring village who had approached him wanting to marry her since she was eight years old. The man had many cows, a form of wealth in the community, and he had been patient enough to wait for Jenny to grow up. She heard her father brag that the man was ready to offer him whatever Jenny was worth in regards to cows and goats because she was beautiful with a lighter complexion, and it was an offer her father couldn't turn down.

The man was sixty years old, and he had seven wives. Jenny heard her father tell her mother that the man had admired Jenny since birth, and he had booked her hand in marriage in secrecy. But the man vowed he couldn't marry her until she underwent the customary rituals. Therefore, her father expected her mother to make the arrangements for the operation to take place without further delay.

After hearing this, Jenny curled into a ball in her bed and clenched her fists. She couldn't believe her mother was falling for what her father told her. She had expected her to put up a fight for her and disagree with her father's wishes, but instead, she sat on the bed ghost quiet, like a scared mouse. Jenny felt little beads of sweat roll down her rosy cheeks like pearls. It was a hot night, and the fire in the shelter had not gone down. As she contemplated what to do, she felt a lump in her throat that choked her, but she tried not to cough. Jenny didn't want her parents to find out she had overheard their plot.

CHAPTER 5

The 'Cut'

It's time to put a stop to this.

After listening to what her parents had planned, Jenny recollected what had happened to her friend Mrembo (a Swahili name for beauty), who had turned twelve years old the previous month during August school holidays. She had a flashback of the women congregating around Mrembo's house. Mrembo seemed unaware of what awaited her as she was lured into the hut and pinned down by the women.

Jenny had gone outside her manyatta to relieve herself when she saw the women and Mrembo enter the hut. They were singing, but Mrembo didn't appear to participate. She seemed to be sombre and bewildered, as she emerged like a sheep driven to a slaughterhouse. Jenny decided to become a detective and followed the congregation, making sure that she didn't look suspicious. She wondered how she could rescue Mrembo or whisper to her to run away for her life.

As she pondered on how she could rescue her, Jenny hoped her friend would figure out on her own that she must escape. Within that moment, she heard her friend scream and shout that she didn't want to be 'cut'. Suddenly, Jenny realised it was too late to save Mrembo. From where she sat hidden, she saw the women pull Mrembo's legs apart and pin them down. Another woman folded Mrembo's hands and pinned them onto Mrembo's chest as Mrembo wriggled but remained glued to the floor and helpless. Her mouth was covered with cloths when she screamed for the women to stop.

Suddenly, the elderly woman lifted an object that resembled a rusty blade in her grimy hand and pounced betweenMrembo's legs.

The woman looked as if she was cutting a piece of meat between Mrembo's legs. Mrembo's scream filled the air, and Jenny could hear the women tell her that she was now a woman.

Jenny felt a chill run down her spine and her blood boil as she breathed heavily. A wave of rage ran through her, as she was unable to defend her friend. However, Jenny knew that, if she had intervened and went ahead with her rescue mission, she would have faced a forced 'cut' with the same blade.

Jenny was pretty sure what was going to follow after the ritual after she quietly listened to her parents talk about her. She had witnessed many young girls go through the practice, and they were married off soon after. Jenny vowed never to fall into the same fate as the other girls, and she was ready to fight for her rights. She wondered why the women subject their daughters to such pain for men's pleasure, but she remembered her mother telling her that no man, not a single one, would marry her unless she was circumcised.

Her heart pounded like an engine when she thought that Mrembo was tortured so that she could get married. She had tried to work out how she could save her friend from being married off, but she had been unable to come up with a solid strategic plan.

As she stared at the women with scornful eyes through the cracks on the wall, she thought she had to act, instead of standing there watching Mrembo go through another brutal act –the act of being forced into marriage. She stormed into the manyatta and screamed for the women to stop destroying young girls' lives. But all of a sudden, she was dragged outside by the women shouting at her, but she didn't give up.

She shouted back at them and asked them why they inflicted such pain on a young girl without remorse. Instead of getting an answer, she received abuse from the women, and they called her the 'uncircumcised one.' Jenny knew that, as long as women fought to continue with the barbaric practices against their daughters, girls' battle for freedom would continue to be fierce combat.

Jenny considered herself a witness to attempted murder. But there was nobody she could have reported the matter. She was aware that exposing the crime to the village elders would have been viewed as going against the family and the traditionally acclaimed customs that the elders refrained from interfering with.

In Jenny's opinion, she didn't have to be circumcised to become a woman. And if the 'cut' transforms girls into women, she preferred to remain a girl for the rest of her life.

She rushed to her house, wondering if she was the next victim. After all, she was older than Mrembo. She asked what crime the young girls had committed to warrant going through such a barbaric practice – a practice that invaded a girl's dignity for the sake of a man. As she prayed for Mrembo's safety, she hoped her friend had not succumbed to death like some girls in the village did during the ceremonial 'cut' and the only way to find out was to walk back to Mrembo's shelter and peep through the cracks on the wall.

As she peered through the holes, she saw Mrembo. Her friend, who was standing up, had a great sob escape her as she covered her face with trembling hands and bleeding profusely. "Phew!" Jenny exclaimed. At least, Mrembo was still alive. The women sang and danced while Mrembo, on the other hand, moved like a snail with a heavy load between her legs. She was expected to rejoice and be merry, but instead, floods of tears gushed down her cheeks.

Jenny felt she couldn't abandon her friend in time of need. She stormed into the hut, but before she reached where Mrembo was standing, Mrembo collapsed to the floor with a thud. The women rushed to her like safari ants, and lifted her onto a goat's skin and fanned her with leaves, to no avail. After about twenty minutes, she came around, but she seemed like jelly, and she was in and out of consciousness, and her voice was fading away.

Jenny knelt beside her friend, and Mrembo slowly reached for Jenny's hand, held it tight and whispered with a trembling voice, "Keep on fighting." With those words, Mrembo's eyes shut, and she took her last breath.

Upon seeing her friend die right in front of her eyes, Jenny trembled as she shouted and screamed, saying, "Murderers, you have killed her!"

As she curled herself in a corner, she thought of the girls who had joined the women outside in dance and song, not knowing they were stepping into the trap of killing their dreams and being killed. She declared that she would not let her thoughts be stolen by those around her.

She began her plans to avoid being subjected to torture. She was deep in thought when a woman passed by and said to her, "We will be celebrating your womanhood soon, as your expiration date for marriage is near." Jenny felt offended by the woman's remarks.

She had just lost her friend. She told the woman she had a choice and was not blinded by the culture like she and the other women were. After all, it was her body, and she was not going to let anybody interfere with it.

27

Jenny pondered whether her mother had discussed with the women the procedure being performed on her. She stared at the woman sternly and shouted: "my flesh will never be mutilated because of a man." Jenny considered every part of her body vital to her and was not ready to let her destiny be planned by her parents or anybody else.

That night, Jenny tossed and turned all night as she sought to comprehend what the woman had said to her. In the morning, she rose before dawn, built up the courage, and decided to confront her mother. Her father had gone to spend a night with one of his other wives, so it was an excellent opportunity to speak to her mother alone. But then she remembered that her father held all the cards, and her mother was just a powerless figure in the home.

Moreover, she found it difficult to believe her mother could do such a thing. But it didn't matter whether she did it or not; her mind was made up. She stormed out of the manyatta and walked towards the cowshed, pondering whether it was best for her to flee from home because she felt unsafe. As she disappeared into the darkness, she heard footsteps behind her, and quickly turned back, she saw her mother creeping slowly towards her calling her in a whisper, "Jenny, Jenny, where are you going? Please come back."

Jenny didn't respond and continued walking straight into the cowshed. Her mother reached up to her, held her hand, and led her back into the hut. She sat Jenny on her bed and shed a tear, still holding her hand. "My gorgeous daughter," she said, "you know you have become of age, and you are about to become a woman."

Straight away, Jenny knew what her mother was about to say, and she listened attentively.

Her mother told her she must be circumcised to earn respect from the womenfolk and acceptance into the community. She said to her with a trembling voice, "It is not my choice, but it would signify your eligibility for marriage. That is what your father wants. Otherwise, no man will take you for a wife, and you will be ridiculed and humiliated by the men and the women in the village."

Jenny stared at her mother and asked her why she didn't object to her father's plan, but her mother gazed at her with eyes filled with tears.

Then all of a sudden, Jenny screamed at her mother that her body was not going to be mutilated for the benefit of a man, and she didn't care whether she was stigmatised or failed to get a husband. She stomped her feet and insisted she wanted to complete her education. Jenny asked her mother why girls had to suffer for the sake of the male. Her mother told her it was a tradition that has been practised for decades, but she was of the generation that could put it to an end.

Jenny wondered what the government was doing to safeguard the girl's well-being and stop the brutality from continuing.

Nevertheless, she realised the administration and police force are dominated by men. She sensed complaining about the cruel treatment is like talking to a brick wall.

Her mother told her that girls from all over the world go through different rites of passage and hardships. The difference is the extent of the adversity women face, which is based on their cultures, customs, traditions, beliefs and, to some degree, protective factors by the families, the communities, the societies, the governments, and the laws of the country. No girl or woman is safe no matter what country she comes from. And a lot happens behind closed doors, and men's domination and control against women always win out.

Jenny listened keenly as her mother narrated to her about girls' lives in different countries. She was not aware that her mother knew so much about what was happening outside the village, as she never ventured out and had been forced to leave school at a young age.

CHAPTER 6

The News

It was written in the newspaper.

Jenny learnt from her mother that her maternal grandfather used to go to town every week, and he would come with a newspaper. Jenny's mum was eager to gain information on what went on around the world, and she would sneak to read the paper when her father was out. She wrote the points that interested her on pieces of paper with charcoal.

However, one day, Jenny's maternal grandmother found the pieces of paper and used them to light a fire. She was not educated, so she didn't know what was written on them. When Linnet found out her papers had been destroyed, she burst into tears. But there was nothing she could do. She was soon married off at the age of ten, and her dream to continue with her writing was terminated.

Jenny asked her mother to tell her everything she knew about girls suffering. Her mother coughed and said she could not remember everything, but she was willing to narrate to her what she could recall. She wanted her daughter to spot the danger signs.

She told her how some girls believe that, if they allow the men to whip them until their backs bleed and cause scarring, it is a sign of perseverance, and they are likely to get a husband. Through the torture, the girls demonstrate they can withstand hardship, and men view it as a symbol of strength and bravery.

Others have their lower lips cut and stretched as much as possible by inserting a plate made of clay. The bigger the plate, the more they are considered attractive and the higher the dowry that would be given when they get married.

Other girls are subjected to incisions on their bodies, sharpening of their teeth, and blackening their teeth or their gums as a sign of beauty to attract men. Others have rings around their necks to give them the illusion of a long neck to enhance their beauty.

Moreover, there are those whose breasts are ironed to cause stunted growth or to make them disappear, for fear the girls' breasts could attract men's lust when they develop at an early age. The mothers think this it's a way of protecting their daughters from the men's prying eyes.

Some girls endure virginity testing to prove their virginity before the marriage. Jenny's mother continued to say, in some communities, menstruating women are considered unclean and contaminated for going through what nature intended. They have to keep away from the house, the animals, and the men, and they are not allowed to eat specific food lest they contaminate it and bring a curse to the community.

Some of the girls live huddled together in degrading conditions until their menstrual cycle is over.

Other women are stripped naked and beaten for wearing skimpy or tight clothes and trousers, while others are forced to cover their entire bodies from head to toe like ninjas. Others are raped and become a laughing stock when they report the crime or are accused of adultery, which leads to honour killing.

Jenny's mother told her, in some parts of the world, girls have no choice of a husband. They get what their family dictate in arranged marriages, and they are not supposed to complain, resist, or choose their own spouses, as any of these things are considered a dishonour to the family.

Some have their breasts pinched, or their appearance disfigured for rebelling against men. In some communities, girls' genitals are cut and sewn together to preserve their virginity for their future husbands, who then cut them open with a knife on their wedding night. Others are snatched by men as brides against their will and pay the ultimate sacrifice for fighting for justice.

After listening to what her mother had to say, Jenny realised it is not only girls in her community that needs rescuing. Other girls are in critical situations too. She asked her mother what torture the men go through for the sake of the women, and her mother shook her head and said, "None!"

Jenny bit her lower lip and said the traditions are dead to her; she has the right to make her own choices. Her mother told her she could not fight a multitude of elements single-handedly.

She yelled, "you support the culture by doing nothing to stop my father from forcing me to go through the 'cut' so that he could hand me over to an elderly man because of cows." But her mother explained to her that the ceremony signified a girl's purity, and it is a way of making sure that females remain faithful to their husbands. It also prevents girls from being ridiculed by other women, and it earns young girls a place in the womanhood in the community. She told Jenny that, without the ceremony, she would be treated as an outcast, and no man would marry her. Furthermore, if she lost her virginity, she was doomed to lead a life of a singleton.

Linnet continued to tell Jenny that, once the rite of passage was over, she would be taught how to become a lady and how to take care of her husband and support her co-wives. She had no chance of choosing her own husband, as she had already been booked for a wife.

Jenny found the practice unjust and repressive to young girls. She told her mother that, if a man was allowed to be with or marry multiple women, a woman should be authorised to do the same if she wished. Her mother stared at her with her hand, covering her mouth. "I can't believe what is coming out of your mouth," she said to Jenny.

Jenny stared at her mother without blinking and said she was never going to be sold like a commodity, and she was never going to become a man's property. Her mother realised she was never going to conform to their way of life. Linnet told Jenny that would ignite conflict between her and her father if his wishes were disobeyed, and it would bring dishonour into the family. Moreover, Linnet tried to convince Jenny to keep the peace instead of resisting because her father had made the final decision, and her failure to obey could lead to shunning from the community, and she had nowhere to go. But Jenny agreed to nothing her mother said to her. She told her mother she lived in the twenty-first century, and she didn't care about the stigma. Her life was her choice.

After her mother failed to convince her, she finally gave in and whispered into Jenny's ears, "Do what you want, my daughter. You have the world ahead of you. Grab it with both hands. The sky is not the limit. Spread your wings and fly as far as you can. You have the strength of a woman.

Nevertheless, be careful. The world can be a lonely place on your own, and the people in it can quickly and unexpectedly consume you. Make your choices wisely with your eyes wide open."

With these words, Jenny knew she had her mother's approval to escape from her village, and she was more determined than ever. However, she had no escape route.

Her father had stopped paying for her education fees when two of her stepbrothers refused to go to an ordinary secondary school and demanded to be sent to a better school that was costly. The sons were the shining armour of the home. Therefore, Jenny was expected to sacrifice her education. Her father claimed he couldn't afford to pay the school fees for all the children, and after all, Jenny was about to have a husband who would take care of her. Therefore, paying for her education was a waste of resources. Her father had twenty children in total between his five wives.

Jenny couldn't comprehend why her education was less valuable than that of her stepbrothers. She remembered the disagreement she'd had with her parents when they'd terminated her schooling. Jenny felt she should have been treated with the same worth as her stepbrothers. Despite her father's refusal to pay her school fees, she continued going to school and told the teachers that her parent would pay soon – until one day the school decided she was no longer allowed to attend lessons.

Warm tears flooded down her cheeks, onto her chin and dripped onto her school sweater. She begged the headteacher to allow her to continue with her education, but he softly told her there were many other children in a similar predicament. Therefore, he thought it would be unfair to let her stay.

A lonely tear rolled down her bright cheeks onto the ground as she walked away with her head held down sheepishly. But as soon as she was out of the school compound, she wiped the tears with the sleeve of her school sweater and decided there were no more tears to be seen.

Jenny treasured education, but she understood that it didn't have the same significance to her father. He had never walked through a classroom door as a child, and most girls in her community are not allowed to have an education from their parents' choice. The one thing the families aspire to for their daughters is a wedding. At the age of fourteen, Jenny was expected to have been someone's wife, but she wanted to break the cycle of discrimination against girls and women.

Jenny taught herself at home, but she found it difficult to get books. All the while, her parents emphasised to her that studies were useless to her. For her, going to school was a waste of time, as she would only end up being someone's wife and staying at home. Jenny's parents told her the most vital education for her was to learn how to take good care for her husband and to keep a house in order. Yet, Jenny turned a deaf ear to what her parents said to her. She vowed to do what it took to get herself out of the culture that denied girls education and stole their innocence.

CHAPTER 7

The Strength of a Woman

The strength of a woman is not about the muscles on her arms but what comes from within, mentally and emotionally: Self-belief that she has the potential and capability to define her future,
Self-belief that pushes her to go to great heights despite the adversities,
Self-belief that she is worth it no matter what other people say,
Self-belief that she is unique, and there is no other person like her, Self-belief that she is the commander of her destiny.

The night after Jenny spoke to her mother, she dreamt of fighting to make a change for girls and women and to educate young boys and men on the importance of working in harmony with the females. She wanted to wipe the girls' tears and see them shine and obtain what they deserve in society.

Her refusal to fall under the control of male dominance strengthened her. She hoped that more females would become presidents and prime ministers of many nations and one day, rule the world.

She wished to have the power to build and control her future. She felt she had the capacity, and nothing could stop her. She was ready to fight to the bitter end for her freedom and worth. She believed it was time women took control of their lives and destinies and that of their children. It was time for women to do what they want and achieve what they desire and no longer depended on men's mercy. She believed a woman doesn't belong in the kitchen, and that she is not a man's trophy to be displayed on a mantelpiece in the home. She has a right to venture into the world and take pride in her achievements, no matter how trivial they seem to others.

If she wants to feel great and do whatever she desires without harming another person, she has the right to do so. And if something makes her feel fabulous, she should do it, but not to please anyone else but herself.

However, she knew her dreams were likely to be quashed by various factors. Childhood attacks, early marriage and pregnancy, lack of education, marginalisation, and socialisation in the family, the community, and ultimately the society.

Nevertheless, she was ready to protect her life and not allow herself to be pushed into a position of powerlessness.

She had witnessed women being crushed because men want them to be in submission under their control, while society watch and do nothing to help and support them. The culture of blame and ignorance spread across the field like a bush fire while the women hung on threads, and they are played like puppets on strings by men every time they resist their advances. Jenny felt it was time to change. Failure to acknowledge she had the strength to break away may have been in her mother's DNA, but it wasn't in hers.

Jenny disclosed her plan to her mother, who agreed to it. But Linnet told her that she was taking a gamble with her life. As Jenny's eyes filled with tears, she slipped a beautiful colourful necklace around Jenny's neck and a bracelet on her wrist as a symbol of strength and as a sign of their closeness. She gave her blessings for Jenny to free herself from the bondage that many girls find it hard to get out of.

Jenny knew it would be difficult for her to return back home once she'd departed. Her father had already made marriage negotiations, and all he was waiting for was her initiation ceremony to close the deal.

Linnet told Jenny her departure would cause anger and strife in the household, as it would bring disgrace to her father. But she didn't care what the villagers would think about the family. She was happy her daughter had the courage that she'd never had to break free.

Jenny made plans to escape quietly and swiftly, but she was also worried about the unknown. However, she was sure there was another world out there. Her idea was to set herself and the womenfolk free.

Despite her desire to be at liberty, she realised she was never going to be 'man-free'. But she was ready to compromise and determine never to submit to a man's demand. She had an image of her ideal man in her head – a modern man who shared responsibilities equally. She understood that this was just a dream, but she didn't want to spend lonely nights alone.

She was ready to venture into the world on her own, like a soldier going to war. She didn't want to leave anything to chances. She knew her fight for freedom was going to be fierce, and she had a long way to go to reach her destination.

She thought about what she would leave behind if she escaped. Her mother was the only person she would miss – her mother, who had endured kicks, slaps, and whipping. Being whipped is viewed as a sign of love by some village women, but to Jenny's mother, it is a way of degrading females. Some believe that, if their men fail to hit them as their neighbour's husbands beat their wives, it is a sign they don't love them.

Some men in her village discuss how they beat their wives, and it prompts others to act aggressively towards their wives; they have to perform the action to demonstrate their masculinity and to command respect from the women.

It had long been a culturally accepted violence and still is. The women endure marital rape and whatever is thrown at them in the homestead. The elders encourage them to be patient and build their homes instead of dealing with their concerns. The blame is always directed at the women for not being the perfect wives and obedient to their husbands.

Married women own nothing, not even their own bodies. Women's bodies belong to the men to use and abuse. The females offer themselves to their men on demand. Sex is rarely a case of loving intimacy. It is a chore that women are expected to fulfil efficiently without fail.

On considering what she had gathered about the women's world from her mother, Jenny felt women should never bend low to a man. But the men have the power. They are protected by the community, the society, the governments, and the law, and they are free to do what they want to women, especially if they are the breadwinners.

In her village, she sensed the women have no voice. Their survival depends on them turning a blind eye to what happens in their lives and pretend to be happy. For some people on the western side of her village, a man has the right to inherit his brother's wife and use and abuse her as he pleases. It is a culture a woman is expected to abide by.

She had watched and ascertained that a man asserts power over a woman in a relationship with little comments here and there. It doesn't matter how small the man is or how large the woman might be. If the poking comments are not stopped immediately, it becomes a part of the man dipping his feet into the water to find out how deep he can go before pouncing on a woman with a punch.

Jenny wasn't prepared to have anybody control her world. She felt she was the boss of her life.

She ruffled her feathers, ready to fight obstruction along her way. Her desire to control her fate was her top priority.

In spite of her fear, there was a sense of excitement. She had no idea whether she was going to be harvesting honey, be stung by bees, or be brought to a dead end by her passion for becoming independent. But she was ready to take the gamble.

She wasn't prepared to give up on her dreams. Her feminine drive spurred her to chase it, whatever the cost. She understood that power acquisition and how she utilised it was everything if she was to succeed in her search for supremacy and independence. Her womanly strength, authority, and willpower, along with support from others were the ultimate weapons she needed to conquer her world. But without the self-belief, she could control the earth and have a balanced compromise and strategy, she knew she was likely to lose the battle for the benefit of another.

Self-acceptance was the first step she took to detangle herself from outside forces that threatened to take over her choice of what she aspired to be. She wanted to cast out the devil of self-doubt and blame and gain a positive impact on her life.

She understood that the forces in the village were geared to destroy her perception of who she was. Therefore, it was crucial for her to understand what she expected and wished for in her life. Jenny decided to move on and discard the negative vibes imposed by those determined to stigmatise and destroy her heart and soul.

The thought of being her own master made her realise that, when women are aware of who they are, they are capable of catapulting themselves into their next stage of development. They are likely to distinguish what is 'normal', recognise the danger signs in their lives and relationships, and take advice with a pinch of salt because not everybody has an individual's best interest at heart.

Jenny felt that some people might try to break others down if they are allowed to do so – to force them to conform. But she thought every person has a right to decide their own destiny. She knew that some people might attack where it hurt. So, it was vital to understand that her personal inner strength was going to be a protective factor in times of difficulties.

She believed that one may be wounded and left with a scar, but when experiences, skills, and knowledge are used wisely, there is a likelihood that the person would embrace self-healing and move forward. She never believed in harbouring negative thoughts that are enforced by others or allowing traumatic experiences consume her inner power or failure to define who she was, where she came from, and where she was going; these, she knew, were recipes for personal destruction.

Her view was that a woman should not let the chains of societal evil and tradition keep her in captivity. She believed a woman can break free if she trusts her inner strength and has faith that her life is not over. It is not a circus, a game of poker, or a commodity.

She was aware of the road she was embarking on was never going to be easy. It could be extended, dusty, muddy, and slippery. But every time it got complicated, it would be crucial to her to gain the courage to carry on and be on the alert while trying different strategies and paths. She wanted girls not to think that failure is the end of their progress in life but to keep working towards their goals and keep moving on in search of their dreams.

She wanted all women to understand that we live in a culture where people with power use their supremacy to oppress others because they can. They make the people who they are supposed to care for feel inferior and vulnerable. The fear imposed on individuals by the systems makes people not question authority, as they are terrified of the repercussions. The culture defines people as not good enough, powerful enough, or safe enough, thus generating self-disbelief.

Jenny decided to have her guard up to protect herself and to safeguard her welfare. She didn't want to leave herself vulnerable and allow the cycle of deceit to catch up with her. Jenny felt like a warrior princess ready to say goodbye to her village life and welcome her new future as her own boss. She decided she was not born to suffer.

CHAPTER 8

The Great Escape

This was the hardest decision of her life but she knew that she had to fight for survival.

Jenny refused to believe that being a woman was a ticket that required accepting inhuman treatment and inequality. As a modern young woman fighting for survival, she thought that leaving her village was the only way to lead her to a new territory and a better life. Jenny planned to disappear without anyone spotting her. She was definite she was her father's future source of income, and he would have done absolutely everything to stop her from leaving.

What's more, Jenny's refusal to be circumcised and to get married would have been a blow to his reputation among other men. She knew her father itched to have his status raised in the community through her dowry payment as the groom to be had promised to pay any bride price for her, as she was a beauty. His reputation as the man who had received lots of cows for his daughter was more important to him than her welfare, and she knew her father would go to great lengths to make sure he married her off. For that reason, she felt she couldn't wait for that time to come.

In the evening when her mother was tending to the animals, she packed one dress, a skirt, a blouse, and two pairs of pants, along with a roasted maize cob and some fermented milk in a small gourd in a black plastic carrier bag. She then hid them under her bed. That night when her mother was fast asleep, she slowly dragged the carrier bag from under her bed and held it tightly against her chest. She then tiptoed quietly towards the door, opened it slowly and gently stepped outside, closing it behind her.

In the darkness, Jenny escaped the impending blockage to her liberation, her father. Everything was ghost quiet and dark, except for the chirping of the crickets and the light from the glow-worms. Jenny felt as if the creatures knew she had a lucky escape.

She moved swiftly with her head held up high. As she disappeared from her hut, excitement ran down her spine, but in the back of her mind, she felt like a fish in a stormy ocean trying to flee to calmer water. She had no idea when the sensation was going to subside. Furthermore, the thought of being caught fleeing made her face tense because every effort she had made would have been futile if she was captured.

She disappeared into the darkness, but she never said goodbye to her family. She was filled with dread when she thought of the consequences she would receive from her father if he discovered her plot and thought it was best to get away without a word when her mum was still asleep.

As she gazed ahead, there was no one on the horizon to come to her rescue. Along the way, she contemplated going back home, but she imagined her future being somewhere else.

She walked through the wilderness, and the idea of a new life spurred her to focus, move forward, and not look back. She was not afraid of the dark, as she was determined to reach her destination come rain come sunshine.

Once she was out of sight, she smelt the scent of freedom, and that gave her the strength and courage to execute her mission. She moved like a rabbit with long strides, glancing behind her to see if anyone was following her. At dawn, the birds began to twit, signifying that morning was breaking and when she couldn't see anyone behind her, she felt secure, and her inner strength gave her the energy to move on.

Thinking about her escape, it dawned on her that no one knows the power of a woman unless it is tested.

She felt her strength hadn't manifested itself in her arms or legs; it was her willpower that had led her to her mission. She supposed she was a quick thinker, and she had a desire to be unrestricted.

She was aware of how everyone in the village talked about her smooth skin, her giraffe neck, her feet like a flamingo, and how she walked like a peacock. She knew she was beautiful, and she imagined her voice to have a silky tone. But she wasn't going to let any man take advantage of her. Instead, she planned to use tactics to force any man who was interested in her to reveal the secrets of male dominance and why men thrived on it.

Besides, she wasn't a fool. She had a computerised brain that was able to process information as quickly as a flash of lightning. She felt like a tornado, ready to destroy whatever stepped on her path. Jenny was ready to rule her world and wanted to be in command at every step of the way.

She considered herself a warrior princess, ready to fight the toughest battle of all time to achieve what she wanted. A voice deep down in her heart spurred her not to be silenced. She refused to allow her spirit to be suppressed like most women around the world and in her village. She desired not to let her power to fall into a man's hand and wished to fight for it, rule, and dominate. She was not ready to give in without a fight.

Jenny was not willing to stop fighting until she achieved her purpose. Her trek through the savannah land towards Nairobi, the capital city of Kenya, was alien to her, as she had never been to the town before.

After trekking for thirteen kilometres following the route, she had heard people talk about under the scorching sun, Jenny felt as tired as a worn-out shoe as she set her eyes on a vehicle approach in front of her. She waved excitedly at it to stop. When it came to a halt next to her, she saw five people in the jeep. The two white females and two males dressed in khaki clothing and hats held large cameras tightly in their hands and smiled as they spotted a zebra with a calf and an antelope jumping about.

Jenny felt beads of sweat roll down her forehead and onto her chin. Her feet had turned a different colour because of the dust, and her mouth felt dry.

The strangers spoke in Swahili. "Jambo!" (Hello), they said.

"Jambo!" she replied.

They then asked the driver in English whether she was all right, and the driver told them she was in her natural habitat, but it was rare to see a girl roaming about on her own in the wilderness.

The tourists stared at her, wide-eyed and asked her where she was going. She told them she was going to visit her aunt in Ngong Town. The travellers told her it was dangerous to travel on her own in the wild.

Jenny turned to the driver and begged for a lift in Swahili. But he didn't respond. Instead the driver told the mzungus (white people) in a native accent that Jenny was asking for a ride. The travellers nodded their heads with a smile, and the driver rolled his eyes towards Jenny and asked her to hop into the jeep. One of the women gave her a bottle of water and some biscuits and told her it was a long way to walk to her aunt's place. But Jenny was not going to see any aunty in Ngong. She was on her way to Nairobi.

At this point, though, she had no idea whether she was following the right track. The people in the jeep questioned her about her family, but she avoided their probing questions.

Before they reached Ngong Town, the driver told Jenny that they had to branch off in a different direction. Jenny told him she was okay, as she was not far from her aunt's house. She jumped out of the jeep, waved and said "Asante Sana!" and one of the girls in the vehicle replied, "Karibu" with a big smile and Jenny walked away. But as soon as the jeep disappeared in the distance, fear crept over her. She walked around, not knowing whether she should turn north, east, south, or west to move towards her destination.

As the rays of the sun submerged within the clouds, she came to the foot of the seven Ngong hills, but she had no idea where she was going. She walked towards the hills, wondering what animals could be lurking about. But she was ready to be devoured by animals rather than be married off to an elderly man and subjected into slavery for the rest of her life.

However, at one point she thought of changing her mind and head on back home to the village, as she didn't know where her destination was going to be. But she knew that she had to continue with her journey and that giving up was not an option.

She had heard the village people say that Nairobi was a city in the sun, a land of opportunities and that it was like being in a different world and that was precisely where she wanted to set her home. She thought she could capture the hearts of the women with all the technology that was available there and with social media to bring them together to fight this battle of inequality collectively.

However, as she gazed at the foot of the Ngong hills, she wondered how she was going to cross over the valleys to her destination. It was getting darker, and her legs burnt. She thought of seeking refuge, but the thought of it made her heart beat faster when she thought of being cornered by wild animals alone in the dark.

Nevertheless, she took shelter near a bush and placed some leaves on the ground to make a bed.

At that moment, her stomach rumbled. She remembered the roast cob and the milk, and she felt she could now eat and drink in peace, but still, the thought of wild animals roaming in the darkness made her stomach churn. She scoffed the cob and drank the milk and then laid her head on her bag.

But as she was about to close her eyes, she heard the sound of movement passing by. She closed her eyes tightly and curled herself into a ball. She said her last prayers as she imagined a lion leaping onto her and tearing her flesh into pieces. But after a few minutes and nothing had happened, she slowly opened one eye and then the other eye and realised it was all in her mind.

The night seemed very long, and she only managed to steal small catnaps, as she believed the animals laid low, watching her ready to pounce on her.

As the morning broke, she was relieved that nothing had happened to her throughout the night. But she knew she wasn't out of danger yet. She still risked meeting people who knew her family. So, she chose her routes wisely and hiked the hills, trying to figure out which side Ngong Town was. She was determined to succeed in her journey.

As she climbed to the top of the hills, the fresh breeze blew onto her face, and as she admired the environment, she was mesmerised by the view. She never knew any other land apart from the area she was born in. Therefore, she certainly didn't know how beautiful other parts of her country were, and it was spectacular. As she surveyed the rift valley and turned to her right, she felt hypnotised by its natural beauty. She then turned to the left and saw what she believed to be the city of Nairobi in the distance. At last, she could breathe. But she was not out of danger.

CHAPTER 9

No Time to Rest

At times, we must ignore the desire to stop and have a rest, as we have important things we must think about.

Finally, Jenny saw a path and followed it without knowing where it led. She wondered whether eyes were lurking about as she walked majestically, telling herself that she walked among the wild animals, and the path was nothing compared to the plains. At long last, Jenny saw a glimpse of life. But in the back of Jenny's mind, her safety was paramount, and as she looked ahead of her, she saw a cave and wondered whether it was a good idea to have a rest inside it. On second thought, she decided she would be wasting valuable time; she wanted to reach her destination before dark.

As she walked through the trails, she saw a magnificent waterfall, and ahead of her, there was an arrow sign saying "Welcome to Oloolua Nature Trail" on a slab of metal which was attached to the ground with a long and thin metal pole. She covered her mouth with her right hand, her eyes fixated on the scenery. The waterfall fascinated her, and she couldn't figure out how the water fell from the rocks. She thought the place was magical, but all she needed was a drink of water to quench her thirst. She bent over to the flowing water, scooped some water with her hands and drank it. She then washed her face and wished she had time to submerge herself in the freshwater. But the journey ahead of her playing in her mind, she had no time for that.

Soon Jenny lifted her head and opened her eyes, but suddenly someone approached her from behind and tapped her shoulder. She jumped up as she set her sights on a figure. Jenny had no time to run or scream, as a tall, dark-looking man stood next to her glaring at her. As she stared back at him, her body shook like a leaf. But with a closer look at the man, she concluded he was harmless, as he smiled at her, but her heart pounded like an African drum.

The man greeted her and asked her what she was up to. Jenny told him she was on her way to Ngong Town to visit her aunt, but she had lost her way. The man told her not to worry, as he was heading that way.

She had avoided walking in the open to avoid meeting people who might have known her from the village. However, she needed direction, and she had no choice other than to follow the man. She made plans along the way on how she would tackle him if he attacked her.

The man asked Jenny about her background, but she didn't want to give too much information or disclose her mission to him. Nevertheless, the gent was kind enough, as he took her to the town centre and left her at a spot, he believed she was close to her aunt's house. When the man disapeared, Jenny sighed with relief and said, "Phew!" She had faith that her lucky star was shining above her, and she was out of sight like a flash, and she thought she'd had a lucky escape.

Soon, she stood on the side of the main road looking left, and right and before long, she saw a man hanging from a matatu (public transport) door shouting, "Nairobi! Nairobi!" Jenny quickly ran to the matatu. And the man shoved her through the door and asked her to move to the back seat. He then slapped the side of the matatu and shouted "Twende!" (Let's go)! With that, the matatu zoomed off.

With every minute that passed, Jenny knew she was getting closer and closer to her destination, which seemed so near yet so far away. A few minutes later, the man collected the fare from the passengers wrapping the notes around his middle finger on his left hand. When he reached to a European man sitting in front of Jenny, he shouted "Mzungu, pesa!" (white man, money)! And when the tout got to Jenny, she stared at him blankly. The male glared at her and shouted, "Pesa, pesa!" (Money, money)! But Jenny shook her head and said she had none. The matatu conductor shouted at her and asked her to pay up or get off the matatu. Jenny gazed around at the passengers sheepishly before the matatu came to a halt. The conductor asked her to get off, but a woman sitting next to Jenny said, "Nitalipa" (I will pay). The tout with a face like thunder told Jenny not to board a matatu without fare again. She nodded her head sheepishly and thanked the woman.

Jenny had planned a strategy of escape, had calculated in her head how it would go. But she had no idea the hassle she would have to contend with to reach her chosen place. Furthermore, she had no clue where in the urban she was going to land.

Her picture of the town was just an imagination. She had heard people from her community say that life there was like living on a different planet, and there were job opportunities everywhere. She already knew how life is for women in her neighbourhood, but she wondered whether it was similar in Nairobi.

She thought she was lucky to have had the courage to pursue her liberty. Her journey to Nairobi wasn't as smooth as a waveless sea. And when she arrived in the inner-city at noon, she was met by other challenges, and she had nowhere to go.

CHAPTER 10

The Queendom is Near

Jenny discovered there was more to city life than glitz and possibilities.

Jenny arrived in the capital city when the sun shone like there was no tomorrow. It was August when she should have been on school holidays.

Now here she was, alone in the vast metropolitan area, dying for a drink to quench her thirst and for something to quieten her growling stomach.

Furthermore, she didn't know in which direction she should head. Urban life was something she had never experienced before. She saw no cows or goats roaming about, and most of the paths were covered with concrete and not like the dusty, muddy roads in the village.

Before long, she found herself ducking the passing cars left and right as they whizzed past her, hooting loudly as she crossed the road. She suddenly froze in the middle of the way and contemplated whether to step forward or backwards before a driver shouted to her face with a loud voice, "Ondoka barabarani wewe mwanamke mjinga!" (Move out of the road you, stupid woman)!

She had never crossed so many tarmac roads before, and she could see the drivers pointing at something, but she didn't know they were aiming at the traffic lights. It was her first time ever to see such views, so she didn't comprehend what they were for.

She remained glued in the middle of the road until she saw the cars stop abruptly and people walkpast them slowly.

She had never seen so many vehicles, let alone traffic lights. In her rural community, there was only one rusty car that belonged to the neighbourhood chief, and it remained neatly parked near his manyatta; it had not moved for two years.

All around her, Jenny saw tall buildings in every direction. She marvelled how people could build such tall buildings that seemed to reach to the clouds. She stared at the people rushing past each other without acknowledging anyone, apart from occasional smiles.

Jenny had no idea who to approach for directions as she didn't know exactly where she was supposed to be, as the people walked past her, gazing at her as if she was an alien.

After watching the public go by, she looked around her and realised she was dressed differently than everybody else. Jenny was dressed in a red, white, and a blue shuka (fabric) with the necklace and the bracelet from her mother, and she walked barefooted. The town women dressed in colourful miniskirts, tight trousers, and long dresses. And they strode past each other swaying their hips with stilettoes that elevated their backside, making them look like the Himalayan Mountains, and the shoes made a clicking sound that echoed on the pavement, announcing their presence.

The carrier bag Jenny held contained her worldly possessions, which were folded neatly. She clasped it against her chest as she walked around the city in circles. She found the capital so different from the quiet environment she was accustomed to. It was full of life, multicultural with diverse cultures, many destinations, and a lot of noise and fumes from the cars.

Jenny compared her life in the village to what she saw in the city and wondered why it was different from the people in her settlement. She thought about how one place could have so much, while her village is stricken with poverty, and clean water is as rare as a diamond.

Nevertheless, she appreciated the vast space and fresh air the rural community people have. She acknowledged that life is different, but the people in her area don't have to dodge cars or people on the streets.

In the village, there is crisp, fresh air, apart from the fumes from the firewood. The thought of it choked Jenny up and tears dripped down her bright cheeks like pearls.

She quickly found out that the city is not as glamorous and peaceful habitation she had visualised. The pace was too fast for her, but she had to adapt to survive.

Jenny thought everything she needed to establish herself was available in the city, but she hadn't figured out how and where to get what she wanted.

She walked around the town, looking for somewhere to rest her aching feet and find shelter from the sun. But there were no trees in sight. However, further into her search for a resting place, she saw what seemed like a garden. There were flowers, bushes and people spread on the green manicured grass under the jacaranda trees sheltering themselves from the scorching sun. She heard people call the place Jeevanjee Gardens.

CHAPTER 11

Jeevanjee Gardens

A place to rest their tormented souls.

As Jenny approached Jeevanjee Gardens, she eyeballed around her to see if she could ask someone for a place, she could get some water. Finally, she set her eyes on a female who appeared dazed, and her eyes transfixed into space.

Jenny took slow steps towards the woman and said in Swahili, "Habari yako" (How are you)?

The woman gazed at her and said, "Mzuri" (Good). After that, the lady stared into space, absent-minded with no further word.

Jenny didn't know how to start a conversation with city people, as everyone seemed to mind his or her own business. But she asked the woman for permission to sit next to her. The female glanced at Jenny with no smile on her face and shyly said, "Okay."

Jenny sat down, wondering what to say next. She was itching to tell the woman her story and seek help from her, but she kept on scratching her head every time she thought about it. The woman finally looked at Jenny and asked her name and where she was from. Jenny replied and asked her the same questions. The lady introduced herself as Rosie Wambui. It was an opportunity Jenny was waiting for – a chance to narrate her story.

Soon Jenny found out that, although they came from different tribes and places, Rosie's and her plights were similar. Both young women had escaped their homes.

Rosie told Jenny that she fled from her village when she had seen a woman who acted as the local surgeon in mutilating the girls' genitals sharpen her knife for the trade with Rosie's mother standing beside her. The woman and her mother had spoken in low tones, and she'd heard them talk about performing the operation early in the morning the following day.

Rosie told Jenny she had witnessed many young girls being led to the riverbank early in the morning. There, some women laid banana leaves on the grass for the girls to lie on. She'd observed the girls being dipped into the freezing cold water and left there for a few minutes before they came out shaking like a leaf. They were then laid onto the banana leaves and pinned down by several women. The girls screamed, and the echoes of their cries could be heard from a distance.

Rosie said she'd heard the sheer agony in their voices. She didn't want to go through similar torture because she didn't see the point.

However, her mother had insisted – she had to be initiated to obtain respect from women and enable her to get a husband.

She'd heard her mother and her aunt plan with the village surgeon, saying they were ready for her rite of passage. Rosie said she was thirteen years old at the time, and she had refused to be initiated. She overheard the women say they had to lure her to the river in the morning. The cold water was the anaesthetic she was expected to get before her operation.

She listened to her mother tell the women that her suitor was waiting. The man was eager to take her as a wife as soon as she was circumcised. Her future husband was a local widower with two young children, a two-year-old boy and a girl who was one year old. Therefore, she had assumed she was going to be the children's stepmother.

She had told her mother she wasn't going to settle down as a child bride. She wanted to continue with her education. She wanted to become a doctor. She didn't want to end up at home with a man who was old enough to be her grandfather and two young children to look after. She realised her dreams were about to be dashed and decided she had to act fast.

Rosie told Jenny that the night before the initiation ceremony, she came up with a plan to run away from her home and find a new life.

At midnight when everybody was fast asleep, she slipped out of bed, making sure she didn't wake up her younger sister, with whom she shared a bed, and walked like a chameleon, tiptoeing towards the door. Her heart throbbed as she grasped the door handle and opened the door slowly, making sure the hinges didn't click, and then closed it behind her.

When she stepped outside, their dog Simba barked in its kennel. She walked straight to it and whispered, "Stop barking. You will ruin my plan. I will be back soon." Rosie had a feeling Simba understood what she said, as the dog kept quiet and wagged its tail.

On the night, the moon was bright, and it enabled Rosie to find her way quickly. She walked hastily through the maize plantation until she came to a dusty road. The road was familiar, but there was no vehicle to take her to the village town centre to board a bus to Nairobi.

She told Jenny she had never been to Nairobi, but she had heard rumours it was a hub of opportunities.

She disappeared into the distance away from her house and found shelter between the banana stalks on a farm. She cut some banana leaves and used them for a bed and cover for the night.

The clothes on her body were her only possessions. She told Jenny that, as she closed her eyes, an owl sheltering on a tree nearby hooted continuously as if it was warning her to get out of its territory. She wished it would stop.

In her township, an owl hooting meant terrible luck. She wasn't prepared to have that. She prayed to reach her destination safely, but the night dragged on. She tried to keep herself warm by curling herself into a ball.

It was the month of June, and the cold wintery weather near Mt. Kenya, a snow-capped mountain, struck through her bones. She struggled to snooze, and when she finally did, she dreamt of a new life in the city. Then again, when she woke up, she wondered how it could be possible; she was just a child with no money and a slim chance of furthering her education.

Early in the morning, she walked through the coffee plantation imagining the magnificent scent of the drink she longed for to keep her warm. But she had no time to worry about quenching her thirst. The one thing that was playing in her mind at that moment was making it to the town centre.

On her way to the centre, she knew her mother would be awake, preparing for her big day. The women in the village had been notified of the occasion, and she knew they would be waiting to celebrate her rite of passage to womanhood with jubilation, filled with songs, dance, and ululations.

At such events, the food was plenty. The women volunteered to prepare traditional food made of mashed maize, beans, and potatoes, with roast goat's meat and stew. The men brewed muratina (a classic wine in central Kenya made from fruits from the Kigelia Africana tree, the sausage tree) with honey or sugar and drank not in china cups or wine glasses, but in cow horns, the Kikuyu traditional way.

As Rosie pondered what her parents might have thought of her once they discovered she had disappeared, she had the call of nature and saw a pit latrine ahead of her. She wished she could dip herself inside it and go, but she felt the opening was too small to fit her body. And on second thought, she told herself, her life was also excellent and precious to go to waste.

She decided to travel to the town centre, but it was miles away, and she had never been there before, but she was determined to have a different life than to be a young bride.

She realised it had been easy to escape, but now she had no idea where she was going. As the daylight dawned, she ran like a cheetah through the coffee, banana, and maize plantations, looking behind her in case she was being pursued. She knew that everyone in the village would be searching for her, and news of her disappearance was likely to spread like bush fire. It was her big day after all.

Rosie arrived at the village shopping centre sweltering and panting like a dog after running for miles, even though there was no sun. She scanned around her, hoping she would never come face-to-face with people from her area. The village people knew each other. Hence, she was aware they would have known about the initiation ceremony, and they were likely to question her if they spotted her.

She wondered which buses went to Nairobi. Then she heard some bus conductors at the bus stop shouting, "Nairobi express!" There were three bus conductors, all yelling, "Nairobi express!" Each conductor was telling the people his bus was a smooth runner and was almost full and ready to leave. She had self-talk on which bus to board but remembered she had no bus fare. Her next move was a blur, as no bus conductor would have allowed her to travel for free. She looked around bewildered which plan was the best.

As she contemplated her next step, a woman dressed differently from the rural women approached her and introduce herself as Sasha Fierce. The lady asked Rosie her name as she shook her hand. And as Rosie moved closer to the woman, she noticed a strong smell on

Sasha's clothes. Rosie couldn't figure out how a person could smell that nice. Rosie was only accustomed to the smell of smoke from the fire and animal manure.

She told Jenny Sasha looked white, but she didn't seem to come from European descent. Her appearance appeared to be of a native with a strong accent. Her shoulder-length straight blonde hair looked like a horsetail, and her face was caked with makeup. Her long thick black eyelashes flashed like a fan – whoosh! She wore red lipstick matching her nails, which looked like claws.

On a closer look, Rosie noticed Sasha wore a pair of tight ripped blue jeans with a red top and red stilettos that were six inches high. Sasha's type of dressing was alien in Rosie's village. Men wore trousers and women wore long dresses or skirts and covered their hair with colourful headscarves.

Sasha didn't waste time. She asked Rosie who she was with, and Rosie replied, "I'm alone." Immediately, Sasha told her she was looking for a housemaid. Rosie, she said, was the perfect person for her. Rosie jumped at the opportunity and thought, what a lucky star. She told Sasha she was actually searching for a job in the town, and Sasha grinned. "Perfect!" Sasha said. "You have the job now."

Rosie knew that gaining employment was the only way she could save money to pay for her education. It was the only hope she had of escaping being married off and of gaining the freedom that would lead her to her future. Without wasting time, she and Sasha boarded the Nairobi express bus to the city.

As soon as they sat down, Rosie immediately began to narrate her story to Sasha, but Sasha asked her to tell her later. She assured Rosie she would protect her, look after her, and take her to school. Rosie beamed and clapped her hands. She considered herself lucky. She was finally going to continue with her studies and her quest to become an independent individual. Rosie thought meeting Sasha was the best opportunity ever. Sasha also complimented her on her beauty with a grin and told her everything was going to be okay.

When they arrived in the city, Sasha made a phone call from her slick mobile phone. Within twenty minutes, they were picked up from the country bus station by an expensive-looking car that took them somewhere. When they got to their destination, Sasha switched on something, and the gate to the house opened itself like magic. As the car drove through the gate, Rosie set her eyes on an enormous garden with bright coloured flowers everywhere, and there was a big white house in front of her.

When they entered the house, she expected to be asked to get to work straight away, but instead, she was asked to make herself at home. She was then given a change of clothes and asked to have a bath. She waited for Sasha to warm some water in a pot for her. But instead, she was led to a large bathroom with a vast white basin in the centre.

The bathtub was filled with warm, soapy water that sprinkled from the sides. The bathroom wall was as smooth as marbles, and its size was four times the size of her bedroom at home. After she stepped out of the bath, she was given a tour of the house. She found the rooms enormous and magnificent. Everything seemed to fit in its place, and nothing looked cheap.

The dining table had beautiful flowers in vases that filled the air with a pleasant aroma, and the size of the house occupied by a single person took Rosie's breath away. She had never been in such a house. Sasha told Rosie that she could one day buy a house like it if she worked hard and remained a good girl.

Rosie believed she could achieve anything, and seeing the kind of lifestyle Sasha led, she was more determined than ever to put effort into whatever she did and to plan a rescue mission to save her younger sister from the barbaric tradition she had escaped from. She had promised herself she would not throw her life away.

On the first night, Rosie said that her bed was fit for a princess. The following day, she expected to be asked to get to work around the house. But she was invited to relax. For three days, Sasha served her whatever she wanted. She wondered what work she was employed to do as the rooms were immaculate and spotless. As luck would have it, meeting Sasha was like winning a lottery.

On the third day, Sasha took her shopping and helped her buy lacy lingerie and clothes that would have been frowned upon in the village. She then transported her in a different car to an unknown destination, where they were met by a male who had his eyes transfixed on Rosie. The man looked her up and down and gave Sasha a wink and an envelope. Sasha glanced at her, gave her a smile, and told her to be a good girl. Before she understood what was going on, Sasha got into the car and drove off. She was left glaring at the disappearing car, clenching onto the shopping bag. That was the last time she saw Sasha.

The man then pulled her hand and dragged her to the house, looking as if he was spitting fire. He ordered her to enter a room, where she met other young girls who appeared shaky. None had smiles on their faces. That was when she realised, she had been dumped, and her life was in danger.

The man told her not to have conversations with the other girls, who communicated with her through gestures. She realised the girl's faces lit up simultaneously when a particular man came into the room. The man had a deep voice, and it seemed like he had a switch that controlled the girls whenever he was present.

Rosie tried to question what was happening, but she was told to keep quiet. The girls whispered to her never to ask anything if she wanted to survive and not to talk to them in the men's presence.

She stared at the girls and saw some of them move like zombies. Also, they had injuries on their arms and legs. Little did Rosie know, soon she was going to join them, and her three-day princess crown was about to be stripped from her.

Before long, she was expected to commence her services. She was given lacy lingerie and stilettos, similar to the ones Sasha had bought for her, and she was asked to dress up and service her first customer. She dragged herself along in stilettos as the man with the big voice pushed her to a room where she saw a man spread himself on a bed waiting.

She quickly ran back to the door, screaming, but the man with the big voice landed a mighty slap on her face. All she could see were stars as he pushed her back into the room. Her hands closed into fists, punched and kicked the man, but she couldn't match his strength as he whacked her on the face, and her screams seemed to go nowhere.

The house was soundproof. As a result, no one heard her shouting at the man in the room as he wrestled her and beat her up, leaving her entire body bruised and aching. Rosie fought back like a cat until the male gave up and said he would have to get his money back.

She later learnt the man with the big voice was called 'Big Daddy', and he was the owner of the enterprise.

Each girl had her own cubicle, where men came in and out during the day and at night. Rosie couldn't comprehend why a human being could do such a thing to people's daughters.

She fumed, and her nostril flared as she questioned where those in authorities were to rescue them. Most of the time, Rosie blacked out, exhausted and sore. Whenever she screamed, she received beatings from the men and her owners. That's when Rosie realised Sasha had sold her into sex slavery. She was now the man's property to use and abuse.

To survive, Rosie had to bear the pain, as crying did not help her. But she never lost hope of one day finding another opportunity to escape. However, there was no way she could survive, as the premise remained guarded twenty- four hours.

She saw money from her multinational clients' exchange hands with her masters before her services. She wondered whether the men were fathers to young girls and how they would feel if their daughters were subjected to such degrading treatment and torture.

She recollected how some of the men's breath smelt like sewage, making her feel like her stomach was forcing food out through her mouth. She felt their massive bodies crush her frame beneath their sweaty armpits as they heaved like wounded hippopotamuses. They showed her no mercy, despite her cries for them to save her.

Her experience made her doubt whether running away from the village was the right move, and she believed she might have tolerated life as a child bride better than enduring the situation she was in at the house of terror.

Rosie told Jenny that, at that moment, she didn't know what was right for her anymore. She had lost the will to live because it seemed there are men traps everywhere, and the women act as bait on behalf of them to capture the girls.

She couldn't stop pondering why women collaborate with men to oppress girls and their fellow women instead of saving them from the lion's mouth.

She wondered how women could liberate themselves if they are not willing to work together to keep the next generation of upcoming young women safe. She marvelled at what the women in power and governments are doing to fight for young girls' lives and women's rights.

Deeply in thought, she remembered how she endured enslavement for ten years, only securing her freedom as she was considered too old to be in the house of horror at the age of twenty-three. She was driven to the city centre at midnight, blindfolded and dumped at Jeevanjee Gardens. She stated that she trembled with terror, thinking the men were going to take her life away in the darkness.

After a man dragged her out of the car, she heard the vehicle zoom off. She remained standing still like a statue without attempting to take the blindfold off thinking someone was keeping watch over her.

However, after some time, she thought she had to do something. She pulled the blindfold off and found herself standing alone. She walked to the garden and curled herself onto the cold bench, and warm tears rolled down her cheeks.

In the morning, she stared at the people walking through the park with her mouth tightly closed, wondering whether anyone would notice her. Every time she saw men glare at her, her heart missed a beat, and she didn't know who to trust. Rosie told Jenny she had sat on the bench for hours, not knowing what to do.

Rosie said before she left the dungeon, she was given a substance which she was often forced to drink by her captors. When she woke up at the park, she felt woozy as its effects wore off and she had a hard time picturing the dungeon in her mind.

Although she was free at last, she felt her ordeal was not over yet. It was just the beginning.

Jenny gave Rosie a tight hug with tears rolling down her cheeks and thought that Rosie had a close shave.

Jenny was gobsmacked and remained tight-lipped for a while, but then she told Rosie to stay firm and to keep the fire for her self-determination burning.

Jenny later came up with a plan to do something. She felt that, with the aid of other women, she and Rosie could conquer the world. She clenched her fists, stomped on the ground, and shouted, "Damn!" She would never have imagined that a woman would entrap Rosie and subject her to such ordeal. The realisation that women work in partnership with the men to torture other women, instead of redeeming them, made her stomach churn.

CHAPTER 12

Social Justice

'Survival for the fittest.'

A woman sitting near Jenny and Rosie stared at them, and when Rosie finished narrating her ordeal to Jenny, the female approached them and introduced herself as Diana. Her forehead creased as her eyes narrowed and told the girls that she was sorry to hear their predicament and offered to assist them.

Immediately, Rosie curled up. The flashback to the day she met Sasha came flooding back, and the memories tortured her mind. Rosie stared at Jenny and shook her head. They told Diana they didn't need help, even though the sun was setting. Diana told Rosie they could report the matter to the police station, but Rosie said, "What is the point? I can hardly recall where Sasha lived or the route to the dungeon."

But the lady persuaded her, and she finally agreed. Diana decided to seek justice for Rosie. She felt that the police with their 'long arms' were capable of catching the perpetrators and punishing them. She wished that the officers would achieve justice for Rosie and help other girls trapped in a similar predicament, waiting for someone to rescue them.

Upon their arrival at the police station, Rosie was interrogated by the police. She could see the cops smirking and others laughing as she narrated her nightmare. She heard some of them whisper that she must have been a slut or she asked for it. Hearing those in authority talk like this was the last straw. This wasn't what she expected from those who she thought would protect her and who regarded their service to humanity as paramount in promoting justice to the powerless.

Diana shouted at the officers and told them they should be ashamed of themselves for humiliating Rosie instead of helping her. She felt the culprits should have been hunted and made to pay for their evil deeds. But instead, Rosie was ridiculed and felt as if her ordeal was justified. Diana apologised to Rosie and Jenny for leading them somewhere where she had thought they could get justice. The police threatened to lock Diana in the cell for public disorder and for disrespecting the officers as she continued shouting at them and she couldn't care less.

To avoid more issues, the girls dashed out of the station, holding each other's hands. Jenny clenched her fist and shouted, "the men win yet again!" Jenny felt her heart pounding, and she threatened to storm back to the police station and give the officers a piece of her mind. But Diana held her back and told her she was only going to cause more trouble for herself.

Jenny appeared older than her age, so Diana knew the officers would have treated her as an adult.

The encounter confirmed for Jenny that women are not safe within their families, in their homes, in their community, or in the society, and the law enforcers have no interest in protecting them against abuse. She felt that women have no secure place where they can enjoy the same independence given to men no matter how much they pretend they are okay.

Diana shed a tear. She didn't know what to do to get fairness for Rosie, and money was scarce to seek a lawyer. The only option Diana had to help the girls were to take them to her home. But the girl's hearts pounded when she mentioned she could take them to her house.

Nevertheless, they knew they had nowhere else to go, and their families and the judicial systems were against them. So, they agreed to stick together and support each other. At Diana's house, Rosie and Jenny felt unsettled. They remained alert at all times, ready to thwart anything sinister that might happen.

But after living with Diana for a month, without any harm coming to them, they relaxed and trusted her.

But still, Diana felt something bothered Rosie. She kept to herself and shuddered when she thought of venturing outside on her own.

Diana told Rosie she could get someone to help her with her concern. And that was a turning point for Rosie's recovery; with help, she learned to cope with her phobias and overcome her experiences. After some time, she felt ready to go to a dressmaking college as she wasn't ready to go back to her parents, and Diana agreed to pay for it.

Jenny's passion was to go back to school; she felt that education was going to give her the platform she needed to empower womankind. However, Diana's finances were limited. Still, while she couldn't afford to accommodate both girls and take care of their education, she was determined not to let them down.

As a survivor of domestic violence, Diana understood what the girls were going through. Diana had no peace in the countryside in her first marriage for her failure to have children. Her husband regarded her valueless, and her in-laws viewed her as unworthy of their son's love. She told the girls the breakdown of her marriage had made her feel ashamed to go back to her home county, due to the stigma of barrenness. The accusations were thrown at her by her in-laws and her family – that she had failed to maintain her marriage.

The blame made her feel she was at fault. She told Rosie and Jenny she had to run to the city hoping to start a new life.

However, life had been a roller coaster, and her survival depended on her alone. She lived in the slums and took any jobs she could get, including washing people's clothes to pay rent for a single room made of poles, mud and corrugated iron sheets for the roof.

She slept on the cold, dusty floor before she saved enough money to buy a single mattress. It was the first time she had fended for herself, as previously she had been wholly dependent on her husband.

However, she worked her way through and acquired a permanent job in a factory where she was still working. She had considered adopting a child, but her experience and lack of financial stability left her unable to do so.

She later met a man who she felt treated her right, and wedding bells followed after six months of courtship. She was surprised to conceive very quickly, soon after her wedding, as she had accepted a life without holding a child in her arms.

In spite of this, when their son was born, her marriage fell apart. She wanted to go back into education in the hope she could attain a decent job, but her husband wanted her to stay at home. She was defiant and didn't want things dictated to her. Violence ensued, and her world became smaller, as she was not allowed to be away from home.

But she went ahead and applied for college and paid the price by being chased out of her marital home and denied access to her one-year-old son.

Her husband's custom dictates that the children belong to the father, and the woman owns nothing in the family.

After the divorce, she left her home empty-handed. Fighting for her rights was impossible. The tradition and the law had trampled on her dignity and worth by siding with her husband. She felt the system had broken her by adding salt to her wounds. She gave up fighting for her child who the husband took to his parents in the countryside, but she kept a single photograph of him that she managed to sneak, with the hope of seeing him again.

Two years after her departure from her husband's home, she met a former neighbour, and she was excited to hear how her son was doing. However, the neighbour looked at her and said quietly, "I am really sorry." Straight away, she knew something had happened to her son. She was told that her son died of malaria when he turned three years old. The husband and her in-laws didn't notify her of her son's death. However, despite her tragedies, her son's spirit lived on. She was determined to stand firm and move on with her life. She wanted to help the girls to do the same.

Jenny continued with her secondary education with the help of a bursary and support from Diana and managed to get to civil engineering course at the University of Nairobi with support from well-wishers. Rosie, on the other hand, finished her dressmaking course and started a new life and settled down with a loving young man on the coast in Mombasa. But Jenny hardly saw Rosie, and she wished that Rosie had finally found love and happiness.

Tragedy would follow. Diana died after a short illness two days after she was admitted at Kenyatta National Hospital with a high temperature of 40 degrees centigrade, and suddenly, Jenny's world came crashing down. She had no idea where to begin tracing Diana's family as Diana had never introduced them to her. But she gained the courage and spoke to some friends. The mates advised her to take the initiative and do what was best for Diana.

With the help of some friends, she buried Diana at Langata cemetery in Nairobi. At the site, there were no dry eyes as the casket was gently lowered six feet under.

Jenny fully dressed in Maasai attire, a beautiful sky-blue piece of fabric draped with beaded ornaments, scoped soil in her right hand

and sprinkled it onto the casket as she pondered on how she was going to move on without Diana. Deep in thought, a woman standing next to her laid her hand on her left shoulder and softly whispered in her ear "I am sorry."

As everyone at the burial began to walk back to their vehicles, Jenny asked to be left alone for a moment. She slowly knelt onto the moist soil next to Diana's grave as tears poured down her cheeks and soaked the ground. Jenny gently placed her right hand onto the red heap of earth and with a trembling voice softly said:"you were my rock Diana, and although you are physically gone, we will always be together spiritually."

Jenny then placed a single red rose onto the earth and softly said "Good-bye mother, sleep tight in peace" and gently stood up, and blew a kiss towards the grave as she walked away.

Soon, Jenny found herself alone and fending for herself. There was no manna from heaven. Friends and strangers were her rescue team and introduced her to all kinds of trades to survive in the bustling city as she continued with her education. However, it was not her choice of life. But she was stuck in a rut, unable to move forward and unable to go in reverse. Nonetheless, she knew her education was her only saviour.

At times she felt empty and found herself yearning for a companion like Rosie's, but she was not prepared to have anybody interfere with her plans of building her castle.

CHAPTER 13

Equality

Equal rights, equal jobs, equal ability to rise through society's hierarchies and equal pay.

Jenny continued with her university studies, and after graduation, she acquired a job in mechanical engineering a male-dominated field. She wanted to accomplish something that may have been viewed as a male profession. She felt what a man can do; there is no reason for females not to try.

However, she desired to get into the political arena and make her voice heard across the valleys. She wanted to lead a political party that didn't marginalise women. One that spoke on behalf of all people regardless of their gender, status and social background. But she had to start from somewhere.

She dreamt of stealing people's hearts through her mindfulness of what matters to them the most – in the united women's queendom. She felt women deserved recognition and emphasised that they don't expect special treatment, but they want equal treatment. They have the desire to be treated with equality in service provisions and allowed to be macho women if they're going to without degrading criticism. Most of all, change is what they want. Women have the power to rule in their homes and on earth.

Jenny aspired to rise to the top and hoped that women would increase to be rulers of nations and let the world see what they can do to bring progress in the countries– she wanted to become a prime minister or a president. She was determined and focused on moving forward in her life. Nothing was going to stop her. But she wondered why the world was full of women, yet women were not represented equally in the governments or family matters.

At her workplace, she was dissatisfied with how the women put effort into their work, but their sweat was never recognised, and their salary never matched their male colleague. The top positions belonged to the men, despite the women having similar qualifications.

It didn't matter whether the women had qualified from Nairobi, Harvard, or Cambridge Universities with masters and PhD degrees in their profession or whether they had the skills and the knowledge required to do the work. Their gender stood in the way in men's eyes.

Jenny felt she couldn't watch what was happening to the women at work and keep quiet because of her gender. For the women to be recognised or receive favours and promotions, they had to be extra friendly to the male counterparts, offer special favours to them, bend over and let the men fondle them with no shame, and brush off comments made about their physical forms.

She refused to be humiliated, and ridiculed because of the size of her breasts, being always told to give up if she couldn't handle the pressure even though she did better than some men.

She refused to be silenced and held down by terror and decided to raise the issue of women being underpaid and degraded in her workplace and the world.

However, her brave gesture didn't sit well with those in authority. As a result, she was threatened she would lose her job because of her constant complaint and her fight for justice. She felt the warnings were meant to shut her up, but she was determined to fight on. However, her quest to involve other women to raise their voices together with her fell on deaf ears. The women at work distanced themselves from her. The work colleagues told her that they had to think about their rent and their bills.

Jenny couldn't believe what was happening. She wondered when women will ever open their eyes and work together to support ladies become independent and win the battle of equality if they couldn't collaborate with each other and go through the journey together – if fear of losing their jobs prevent them from uniting, they will forever be inferior in men's eyes. She felt they would rather have their voices shut down and be stuck in the slavery of the mind and soul than fight for their rights and freedom.

She recognised that fear and oppression play a significant role in condemning people to their situations, and her workmates were those people. Jenny's voice became a threat to the establishment, and as a result, she received a dismissal letter accusing her of inciting her workmates to demonstrate and destruct the smooth running of the workforce. Furthermore, for not heeding the management warnings to keep her mouth tightly shut.

She worked for the firm for two years. But she vowed not to let the sacking push her into depression or drown her sorrows with drugs and alcohol. Instead, the incident made her have a surge of energy. Although her lifestyle changed due to sudden financial struggle, she was determined to fight on.

However, her dismissal intensified her frustration that the women at her workplace preferred to be downtrodden than campaign for equal rights. But Jenny's desire to keep on fighting and put up a stand against the systems remained solid.

Jenny knew the opposition was ferocious, and she couldn't fight alone. Still, she was ready to challenge the systems because she knew the culture as it is currently organised seal the eyes and mouths of women. Therefore, the ladies become part of the problem, and part of the cycle of continued harsh treatment of women. Anxiety and the fear of the unknown weaken them. Some of the females collaborate with the men. The women humiliate and degrades their fellow women who deviate from the norm. The degradation is committed in the name of the call of duty.

Jenny wanted the women to resist gender imbalance in every sector and in the world. And She was eager to end the cycle of injustice, discrimination, and oppressive practices to make the next generation of women feel empowered in every part of their lives. She believed females are no longer living in the yesteryear where the kitchen was their domain, and childcare, and entertaining their men in the bedrooms were their only duties, while the men belonged in the offices and took a newspaper for a company when they arrived home.

She felt it was no longer the time when the men waited for the food to be served at the table and never raised a finger to help at home. Furthermore, once their bellies were full, they hopped onto the bed and spread themselves out, waiting for the women to complete their day's chores before switching onto the night shift of entertaining them. The husbands would then roll over satisfied in their bellies and refreshed and snore like happy cats, leaving the women gazing at the ceiling counting the imaginary stars. The top dog ideology had to go!

Jenny's top priority was the inclusion of women in all the areas in the social order. She believed that a Chihuahua is as good as a pit bull terrier when she thought of the animal kingdom. She considered that women's physical strengths don't match that of men, but she was confident that each has a purpose and is capable of contributing to society. The primary concerns, she believed, should be the ability to do the job required and to get equal pay for doing so. It should never be about gender.

Being dismissed from her job meant she had to move out of her posh area to an affordable one. She thought that, if her fellow workers had fought together, they would have won because many voices are powerful than one.

The situation stressed her out at some point, but she didn't want it to affect her future progress. She hunted for a job for months before landing for a casual one. By this time, she wished to be with someone – someone with whom to share life's burdens.

CHAPTER 14

It's Not a Man's World

A man is nothing without a woman.

Jenny felt it was time to seek someone to fill the hollow emptiness in her heart. She thought that collaborating with a man could strengthen her fight for womankind. Her thought was that it would allow her an opportunity to have a closer understanding of what men really want from women, and what makes them tick. She felt she had a good chance in the city to get an ideal man.

However, she searched far and wide but found no man of her fantasy insight. Although she was never short of admirers, her eyes were focused on a particular sort of man, not a sponsor or a sugar daddy because she never wanted to have a slay queen tag. She wanted a man who passed her tests and shared her principles. But she soon realised that, in the city of dreams, men corrupt women's mind with new technology and gifts, with the desire to control them by providing them with a false short-lived glamorous lifestyle. It was not what she had anticipated in her newfound freedom.

Furthermore, women are not free to dress how they wish. They are labelled as sluts for wearing tight trousers, miniskirts, or cropped tops. They are beaten and stripped naked in the open air. The males pull them apart like a pack of wolves vying for blood on the roadside and at marketplaces while the public watch and laugh.On the other hand, the women whisper in low tones, for fear of becoming the next victims if they intervene. Fear makes them not protect their fellow females, and the authority turn a blind eye to the men's acts of degradation against women.

She witnessed the men assault the girls because of their dress choice. The men dictate how women should dress, but no one controls what the men wear. They can walk around stark naked if they wish, and society would hail them for their bravery or call them insane. Furthermore, displaying their pot bellies in their eyes signify wealth, and when females walk with a swagger in tight clothes displaying their Himalayans (buttocks) swinging up, down, up down they are criticised for attracting male attention and for dressing up indecently.

The men are also free to be with as many ladies as they wish. But when women do the same, they are called a whore, and the wrath of the men befall such women, leaving them bruised and hurting. After all, its men's world and they make the rules.

The men have become morality police, but their morals apply to women and women only. They feel that females have no minds of their own. Therefore, things have to be verbalised to them, and they have to be controlled. If they fail to obey, the males have the right to subject them to demeaning and vicious treatment. Jenny wondered how women could think forward without being given a chance and a platform to raise their voices.

She viewed the men as hypocrites and asked what they would say to women from different countries who go out semi-naked as a tradition, but she knew that they would call it primitive. She realised the city had its set of challenges, and there was nowhere for a woman to hide and live in peace.

Jenny was not ready to let any man get into her mind and destroy what she was working to achieve. She figured she had to work out a strategy to save womankind. But Jenny needed women's support and a man to act as bait for the menfolk. She wanted to gain the secrets of their strength and their insecurities, which seemed to be the most significant disease in the men's world.

She sensed male self-doubt, insecurity and ego is the root cause of their evil acts against women. It isn't because they are physically mighty; it is because they feel women having power is a threat to their ego. Therefore, they have to control ladies to look fierce.

She desired to sweep men like a tornado and weaken their every sense. She regarded them as species of a secret society. Jenny understood it was hard to break into male codes. Their secrets are locked deep in their chests, and it's tough to penetrate them. She felt men expect women to expose their secrets to them while they give nothing away.

She pondered on what the women at her previous job had said to her – that whatever they told their partners was later used against them. Their insecurities about their bodies were something the men used to humiliate and degrade them, a way to keep them on the leash after the honeymoon. Such confessions were also used against them as a weapon to destroy their confidence and self-worth when the relationships turned sour and to bring them down.

But Jenny had the charm of Delilah on her sleeve, and she believed she could conquer the strongest male in the world with her mind. Her view was that men are physically strong but emotionally weak. They can easily be broken when women know-how. It is about cutting the bud before it develops into something else.

Jenny was ready to use weapons that God gave her generously to boost her defence and enable her to squeeze every detail of men's strength out of her imaginary man. However, before she did that, she decided to search for her inner peace.

CHAPTER 15

In Search of Tranquillity

Cool water that runs deep.

Jenny took herself out of her situation to focus on something different in a serene place to open her mind further and figure out what to do next. While she considered her next move, she sat under the shade to escape the scorching midday sun as she admired the tranquillity of the Karura Forest in Nairobi with its colourful natural vegetation. The cool breeze chilled off her body temperature while she gazed at the cold-water flowing from the waterfall with calmness.

Jenny held her cheeks with both hands, wondering why life couldn't flow like a river without the stormy waves. In her dark thoughts, she concluded: There is always someone somewhere who block another person's progress through control, judgements, criticism, injustice, discrimination, and oppression.

As she contemplated what to do next, she looked into the sky and glanced at a beautiful bird with black and red feathers perched on a branch. She thought of the bird's freedom to fly freely without restrictions and wished she could fly like them, without borders and without being afraid of the unknown.

She listened attentively to the bird's melody harmonised with the pouring of the water from the waterfall as it hit the rocks at the bottom and the swaying of the tree branches. It was just like the garden of Eden. She released herself and sniffed fresh air, and immediately, she felt at ease and calm. But something refused to escape her mind.

She reflected on the deeds against women and supposed the Karura Forest and the women had something in common. The fact drew her closer to it. The forest was on the verge of being destroyed by men. But a ferocious fight by a woman erupted as she fought like a warrior to stop the wood from being killed.

The woman was ready to face those in authority, and nothing could deter her not even the heavily armoured guards or the land grabbers with their big watchful eyes. She had a mission to save the forest, and she was unstoppable even when she was beaten, bloodied, and put under house arrest.

She went out there with the strength of a woman breathing fire, but she was not alone. She collaborated with men and women who believed in her course. She wanted to preserve the forest for future generation to admire, for its history, and for the benefit of the environment inspired them to save it from destruction so that it could showcase its beauty to the natives and visitors from around the world. Her determination saved the trees and the vegetations from being wiped out, and she planted seedlings to replace the trees that had been chopped, and the citizens supported her to beautify the area, and now it's just like paradise on earth.

Her efforts would ensure the animals had a place to call home and the people around the world could enjoy the forest's beauty and tranquillity. Jenny thought to herself, isn't a girl's life much worthier of such defence? Why can't we make the earth a paradise for all? Why can't we save our young girls and ourselves? She wanted the world's women to help her fight for their rights and stop the destruction of womankind and strengthen the future generation of girls and boys.

She longed for women to begin growing roots for what they believe in and not back down due to pressure. Although she was ready to fight for the liberation of women and girls – for their ability to choose and for their equality – her power was not enough to fight alone. And she wouldn't have come out unscathed.

She felt just like the trees that were being chopped down. Girls are maimed, murdered, defiled, molested, humiliated, and reduced to zombies, across the globe, and the perpetrators are let loose by the authorities, the communities, and the societies to continue with their evil deeds.

So, had the perpetrators been enabled to continue with their activities of destruction when the administration quietly stood aside as the forest was stripped bare, and those with money and power watched, while the powerless drowned themselves in their tears stripped of their courage and confidence, all the trees would have been entirely wiped out.

Jenny was sure women's rights can be won if females resist oppression, and fight for freedom together, without fear, until their voices are heard across the world. But words alone might never make long-term changes. Women need to act. Her vision was to see a world where the ladies live in peace and enjoy their lives.

She asked herself whether she was ever going to meet the man of her desire. And the more she thought about it, the more her mind told her men are almost all the same, with only a few good ones. Her mind and heart were in conflict, and she failed to comprehend which way was the best to go. She wanted a man she could share everything equally and with whom she could lead a life without restriction.

As she puzzled whether there are really any such men left on earth, she watched behind her and saw a figure approaching from a distance, wearing a big smile. She was unable to tell the man's intentions, but she realised that his eyes were glued on her.

She flushed and looked over her to see if the man was smiling at someone else. But he seemed to focus on her, and she prepared herself for combat. She wasn't takingc hances.

Jenny took men as rivals. She thought they craftily meander into women's lives like puppies with the pretence that they want to be partners. Then, when they'd set roots, they grow horns, and things have to be done their way. When they fail to get what they want, they attack like bulls, leaving women battered, bruised, bleeding, and ultimately death. So, she remained alert at all times.

Jennyreminded herself that she had gone to the forest in search of a serene environment to unwind, not to search for a lover. However, her stroll among the exotic trees of the woods opened her horizon. She felt that, without it, she wouldn't have met and locked eyes with such a figure.

The stranger walked with swagger with calculated steps toward Jenny and looked like a rare hunter hunting for its prey in an exotic environment. Then again, he had no spear, no club, and no shield, the tools used at her home when hunting. Neither was he draped in a bright colourful red, white and blue checked shuka (Maasai blanket) nor was he wearing sandals made out of car tires and his hair wasn't dyed red with ochre and fat and twisted in small braids.

Closer inspection revealed the figure advancing towards her had a stature she had never seen before. The man was tall with muscles in all the right places, piercing blue eyes, tanned skin, and long brown hair. He walked majestically towards the falling water and bent over it.

His flowing hair spread over the cold water, and when he stood up, he wiped his face with his hands and then shook his head spraying the plants with the water from his hair like a water sprinkler. It was a spectacular sight to witness.

The man seemed like a peacock displaying its colourful feathers to entice a peahen. And Jenny's eyes were glued on him, and she thought what a dude, but she didn't want to pay too much attention to him.

She gazed up into the sky, viewed the sun's rays penetrate through the treesas she walked away from the man. As she gently stepped on the dry leaves, she counted the army ants rushing in a row without breaking the chain, as she tried to avoid direct eye contact with the person.

However, every time she turned in his direction, their eyes locked, and he seemed to scrutinise her with a smile. Jenny swung her hips away from him and planned an ambush if she was attacked. She thought he was not the ideal man she was hoping for, but she was mesmerised by his stature.

The man walked straight towards Jenny and stared straight into her eyes with a beam on his face. Jenny saw a twinkle in his eyes before she turned her back on him. A few steps away from the male, she turned to have a quick glance at him and found him still staring at her.

She ignored his advances as he approached her. She assumed he was assessing whether he had found a black diamond without breaking the earth. She knew many men who set their eyes on her were hypnotised by her beauty.

She reckoned God had created her without a hurry, and at the age of twenty-five, she saw no rush to have a partner. But her world had to change for the better. She felt irresistible in men's eyes, then again, she was not ready to be swept like the sand by a hurricane. There was no time to flirt, and putting her trust in a stranger was a dangerous move. She was aware of what this new character was capable of doing without speaking to him, but she didn't want to make assumptions before she got to know him. She had to hunt for her rival tactfully.

While she was not ready to give up her ego, it was critical to soften and let her strength and control determine who ruled in her world in a more compromising way, to maintain equilibrium.

She had to keep the focus on who she was. She was not ready to share her territory with a stranger, but she needed a man on her terms – total freedom and a balancing act. In her mind, she asked herself, "who is this man?" as she watched him stroll away.

CHAPTER 16

The Alpha Male

He travelled around the world in search of his prey.

Meet Johnny, the stunning farm boy who turned into a millionaire mogul. Johnny was an only child, and from the moment he was born, he was adored by his parents. They cherished and treasured him like a prince.

However, his observation in his neighbourhood as he was growing up was that the men spent most of their time doing their things while the women did all the domestic chores. He later realised he was expected to engage in rough and tumble with the other boys. His father told him it would teach him to be a 'man' instead of hanging around his mother.

As a little boy, whenever he got hurt and cried, Johnny heard his father tell him not to be like a woman as he sped to his mother for a cuddle. He wondered what his father meant, and he thought that only women are allowed to cry. He did whatever his father asked because he didn't want to become like a woman.

His father always told him to be smart and robust in mind and never to let a woman rule over him or show his emotions. Otherwise, he would be dumb as a woman. Therefore, he had to prove to himself and to his father, he could assert his powers over the girls. He had to stand up firm and demonstrate to the social order that he was the alpha male.

As a young man, he desired to have control of his life and have his own home away from his domineering father – a kingdom over which he could have an absolute rule. He wanted to be in control and have women worship every footprint he left on the ground.

At the age of twenty-five, he travelled around the world, away from his dictatorial father, in search of an empire he could call his own. He dreamt of being surrounded by women and commanding them as their master. When he began having these thoughts, he wondered whether he was turning into his father.

He remembered as a child his mother shuddered whenever his father shouted, and at times he heard banging in his parents' bedroom after which he could listen to his mother sobbing. He never saw any scars or bruises on his mother, but she always wore long dresses or skirts and long sleeved tops and cardigans.

As time went by, he realised the law of his country was getting more robust, and the women were fighting for their rights. One of his best friends was imprisoned for viciously assaulting his girlfriend, and another onejailed for life without parole for murdering his wife. His other friend paid his ex-wife a hefty divorce settlement and upkeep for their baby.

The friend didn't want to have children, and when his wife had fallen pregnant, he'd tried to force her to get rid of the baby. But she had kept the baby and had filed for divorce.

Johnny wasn't prepared to go through the courts or to jail, but he wanted to have control in his private life and aimed to make the rules in a relationship and gain full respect.

Therefore, he searched for his empire in lands that buzz with different principles, customs, traditions, and authorities than his own – nations where patriarchy rule and laws are lax when it comes to women's affairs.

However, he couldn't find a woman who appealed to him. But he managed to secure a business transaction and got many business associates to work with him.

He anticipated reaching the Promised Land. He couldn't wait to step out of greying cold England and onto the Kenyan soil. This is the land of the wonders of the world, where animals roam freely – a nation that is a hub for pure talents waiting to be discovered.

He wanted to be where he could roam freely like a lion hunting for its prey without the prying eyes of the police. His intentions were close to his heart.

He had been advised by his friends to avoid women from certain tribes, as they are hard to tame and they would milk him dry. Dominating one of them would be like turning her into a lioness capable of fighting back to the bitter end and hit where it hurt the most.

He knew he had to have a woman in his business. A lady to hide the real picture of his trade and for her to work for him as bait. But he had to heed the advice from his friends, as they had been in the county many times. He convinced himself he was not going to leave anything to fate. He had to observe the women's characters before pouncing with his heart towards the unknown.

His last stop was so near but yet so far away. He had wandered into the world, and nothing was going to stop him from getting what he fancied. He was unaware of what awaited him in the Promised Land. However, he was ready to travel for miles and trade the prolonged English cold winter spells for clear warm days with bright blue skies dotted with clouds that looked like cotton wool.

He wanted to witness the pure magical, captivating sunset as it slid warmly into the horizon with its vibrant blue, red, and green colours away from the constant grey clouds in his country.

Without much thought, Johnny packed his bags and flew his nest. It was snowing in the evening, and he couldn't wait to land his feet on the Kenyan soil. Johnny planned to stay close to the locals. He believed that was where he could learn more about the natives. He wanted to be like a nomad and settle where the grass was greener thousands of miles from his homeland, and his mission was clear.

Entertainment by the vibrant cultures, watching the magnificent wildlife and wildebeest migration, and hunting the game wasn't what he anticipated. He was on a mission to track for a different kind of animal. His only worry was going back empty-handed or dropping dead in a foreign land before he conquered his kingdom.

On his arrival in Kenya, to his surprise, he was treated like a king. The grass was even lusher than he had imagined. He was sure he could hunt freely and capture what he wanted. He knew that money talked. He had enough to bribe his way through every situation. He considered the place a playing field where he could amuse himself the way he liked.

He planned to mould a lady like a paper-mâché to suit his eye's desire and his taste. He was not going to settle for less. His powers were limited without an attractive woman to act as bait to attract his prey. That was for sure.

Johnny felt his arrival to the Promised Land was a breath of fresh air. The weather was warm, and he was happy to wear light clothes without worrying about the climate changing withoutwarning like the English weather.

But his journey to the country had a secret mission, and his search had to commence straight away. He decided to stay in a cheap downtown hotel, where he could mingle with the locals. He didn't want to stay in five-star hotels with tourists or be treated or viewed as a tourist.

He walked through the bustling city in the sun, hunting for his soul mate and a woman for his business. To be a perfect match for the job, his woman had to be fierce, intelligent and be aware of her place in the relationship.

When Johnny surveyed the city, he was surprised by what he saw in the surrounding suburbs. It was not what he had expected. He was faced with two different worlds that are separated by roads, massive perimeter stone walls, and iron gates.

Furthermore, he found meandering through the corners in the slums of Mathare more accessible than getting through the gated communities.

He wondered why affluent people locked themselves behind the perimeter walls but realised that wasn't what he had come to research.

Still, he couldn't ignore the leafy suburbs behind the closed gates, with huge mansions, manicured gardens with sprinklers spraying the green grass with freshwater and signs written at the gates'Mbwa kali' (dangerous dogs), they announced in Swahili.

The cars that drove through the gates were the latest models, while in the slum owning a bicycle is like sheer luck. Furthermore, he found out that slum dwellershavesanitation concerns and no tap water in the houses. Sewers meandered like tributaries without directions with gushing murky waterthat smelt like rotten eggs. The children played in the water and picked their makeshift footballs made out of plastic papers with bare hands whenever the balls rolled into the water. Ducks, chicken, sheep and goats drank the water too.

At night, flying toilets in polythene bags flew over rusty corrugated iron sheets rooftops like lightning because it is too risky for women to use the makeshift toilets outside their houses. They risk being attacked and rapped.

In the slums, water appeared to be a treasured commodity, and riding a bike through the shelters seemed like trying to insert a rope through the eye of a sewing needle. It was even harder for Johnnyto pass a crowd without the children running after him calling, "Mzungu, mzungu!" (White man, white man)!

Johnny had thought the division between the rich and the poor in his country is vast but found the slums are very different from the council estates and high-rises in England. He considered the dwellers in the council properties in his hometown as living in luxury compared to what he saw on the outskirts of the city of Nairobi. But the dwellers in both situations are at the bottom of the financial ladder. And separated from the rich by roads and fences.

The politicians visit them during the election campaigns and promise them the heavens. However, after that, the slum dwellers never see the back of the politician's heads again until the next election campaign.

The governments'leaders clearly have no interest in the slum dwellers or their welfare. They areonly interested in the people's votes to keep them in their political positions.

Johnny couldn't comprehend why the slum residents keep on voting for the same politicians when they make no difference in their lives or the community, they live in. But that is the power of politics.Along with illiteracy and lack of thinking outside the box among destitute persons.

In those environments, he found out jobs are scarce, and men and women have no choice of the jobs they wantto do. They do whatever tasks that are available, including emptying excretion from makeshift toilets with bare hands, collecting materials from dumpsites and recycling them for money, washing clothes for people or carving stones in the quarry all day with a homemade hammer with sweat dripping down their foreheads in the scorching sun for a mere two to three dollars a day. Money that is never enough for food, rent, or to feed a family.

He understood the women leave their young children locked in the houses unattendedor with neighbours without food to look for casual jobs, like washing clothes for middle-class people who treat them like slaves for two dollars a day and some work with their babies wrapped on their backs. Their livesare like a merry-go-round financially, and they seem stuck in their situations.

Johnny also discovered there is a wealth of talent in the communities, but the people have no one to hold their hands and guide them in the right direction. There are also some intelligent young people whose lives go to waste due to lack of support.

However, despite the people's circumstances, everyone he met from the shacks smiled at each other, and folks had conversations with their neighbours. He even hadpeople welcome him for a meal of ugali and Sukuma wiki (a mixture of cornmeal and water made with white maize flour and eaten with chopped fried collard green, onions and tomatoes). Eating meat in the neighbourhood seemed like an early Christmas to most families.

He thought of how people in his country don't even know their next-door neighbours, and despite getting things like money, houses, and schooling for their children for free, they are never satisfied with what they getand complain all the time.

Johnny felt that his future partner and Mrs was somewhere in the vicinity. He had no worry about whether she came from the gated community or the slums. But he had to be smart while in his pursuit for his lady.

He encountered many females when he explored his new environment in the city and beyond. Johnny realised the women he met were masters of game-playing, but his queen was not one of them. He knew she was somewhere, and he was ready to hunt for her high and low, not forgetting what his friends had told him about being selective.

Within the town centre, he met females of different characters in night clubsand distinguishing the right one was a task, as they shoved each other out of the way and squeezed in next to him. Some even claimed he was their boyfriend to put the other girls off, even though he barely knew them. He went with his gut feelings; he had decided to stop being too analytical and go with his heart. Nevertheless, none of the girls was what he was looking for. He found them too pushy.

While he surveyed the city of Nairobi, he thought of his wandering habit, which enabled him to encounter different women and left a trail of destruction behind him like a tsunami. He thought of how he runs across the world like a fugitive to avoid the scrutiny of his business. And, he could hear his voice echoing back at him, "Go, Johnny, go!" At forty years old, he knew age was catching up with him. He had travelled across the world, scattering his seeds everywhere. He was now afraid there could be little Johnnies and princesses somewhere without a dad. He didn't want to do that anymore.

He was aware that, to get the woman that he wanted, he had to change his personality and use his looks instead of his power, to disguise his intentions. He knew that ladies fall stupidly in love and attach their hearts to men like leeches, trying to suck the enjoyment out of them. Once hooked, it is hard to let go. He felt it was an ideal formula for a man to assert his authority over a woman.

He had no worry about getting a lady because there were so many women, but there was too little time.

Johnny had been a womaniser, but he found it challenging to keep up with the females in his land. He felt the women had become more outspoken, liberated, and independent. They speak and dress the way they want without a care in the world. Their dress code is their choice. Controlling them is a hard task because those who know the law never hesitate to use it against men. And even if they don't realise it, there are other people ready to corrupt their minds and push them to seek justice in courts.In spite of this,some wouldn't dare to cross a man's path.

Moreover, they have support from organisations and charities and more options than he would have imagined. The phones and the police are within their reach. Unlike in the East, he was free to use the womenright in front of the eyes of the cops.

Johnny moved quickly from one country to the other. He didn't want his business deals discovered by the authorities. Johnny let others do the dirty work for him, while he cashed in the money. He felt that the police were likely to be alerted if suspicious activities were identified by the public. His business was his life, and he thought that having a beautiful, intelligent wife could act as a cover-up.

He sensed that in England, a woman's disappearance was broadcasted on the front pages of the newspapers and the television in twenty-four hours, which gave him restless nights. He loved his peace of mind. He didn't want to worry about when he was going to be caught by the authorities. That's why he loved foreign women. No one would know his secrets.

That was why he thought his only option was to venture to a foreign land, where he could get a woman and have total control under the noses of the communities and the criminal justice system. He knew it was easier to instil fear in a foreign female because the laws in some foreign countries don't care about women. This makes women more likely to do as they are told by their international partners. They have no voice in front of men.

Furthermore, in some countries he had travelled to, the men are scarce. Therefore, a woman would instead perseverebeing dominated by a European man rather than face the stigma of unmarried women and poverty. That was why most of his friends preferred to get their wives from Asia. They knew the women would be submissive and 'good wives', unlike some European women who like to weartrousers and share everything equally.Call it whatever you want, but Jonny called it the Independent women syndrome.

To instil fear, his friends threatened their wives and girlfriends with deportation if they disobeyed them. He found that the females dreaded being sent back to their countries by the immigration officials, especially if they are the source of income for the family back in their motherland. Others were forced to go to work and support the men financially without objection. They had to pay for their men, bringing them to the country.

Therefore, Johnny knew that, whatever he did, the law enforcers wouldn't be quick to act.

In many countries, domestic violence is considered a family issue. The authorities see it as a private matter better left to be settled by the family and the elders.

Moreover, he could bribe his way out of situations. Money talked in his world.

CHAPTER 17

The Mystery Figure

Judging a mysterious love by its cover is a dangerous game.

Jenny's desire to be considered as a human being and not a commodity or a lesser species in society led her to search for her inner potential. She wanted to prove to the organisation she was as good as a man in many ways, but it hadn't worked out how she wanted it to.

She had a strong belief in herself that she could conquer the world. She had walked among wild animals to follow what she believed in her fight for her self-worth and dignity. And to be with a man of her choice.

Jenny had hoped that meditating about her situation could allow her to streamline her future. But she was unable to get the image of the figure at Karura Forest out of her mind. Every time she thought about him or visited the forest, she felt butterflies in her stomach.

On one Sunday afternoon, as she walked around the forest searching for a perfect place to meditate, she failed to recognise what was happening to her body; her legs turned to jelly, and she lost control.

But before she fell to the ground, her eyes locked onto an approaching figure. She realised it was the same man she had seen the previous Saturday and wondered whether the man was stalking her. She told herself that she had not come to the forest to look for a man but to get in sync with herself.

The figure came closer and closer. Jenny couldn't work out why she was affected physically by staring at the stranger. She convinced herself she had to have self-control and not let the physical appearance of the man deceive her.

However, she couldn't avoid staring at him every time he looked away. She had her eyes glued on him as she stepped forward and tripped. But before she landed on the ground, the man ran to her and got hold of her. She got up and smiled as he asked her whether she was okay. Jenny said, "Yes. Thank you," and walked away.

Suddenly, the man held her hand and pulled her towards him. "I think I saw you last week," he said. "Probably," Jenny said.

The man introduced himself as Johnny and asked Jenny what she was up to. "Meditation," Jenny replied. Johnny smiled and told Jenny they could meditate together, but she pushed him away and told him she wanted to be on her own.

It was the first time Johnny had faced rejection from a woman. Nevertheless, he was determined to nail her. He never gave up trying.

They later sat on the grass, and Jenny suppressed her smiles and pretended she had no interest in him, although the attraction was mutual.

During the chat, Jenny failed to comprehend why she was drawn to Johnny so quickly and pondered what was happening. She thought that Johnny had cast a spell on her. Then, in the process of her wild thoughts, she remembered that one of her friends had told her she'd fallen in love with her husband the first time they met.

Jenny didn't want to trust Johnny straight away, but she couldn't resist his charm. Her only way to ponder on what was happing to her was to get away from him.

However, before she excused herself to leave after two hours of talking, he leaned forward and kissed her on the lips. Jenny pushed him away.

It was her first kiss, but she didn't know what to make of it. Johnny figured out very quickly that Jenny was inexperienced in the department of love. Any progressive approach to Jenny seemed like a sign of attack, and she immediately raised her guard. Johnny thought she was the perfect woman that he had been looking for – inexperienced and young-looking but strong-willed.

As Jenny stood up to leave, her legs had gone numb, and she landed back on the ground. Johnny quickly held her, but she gathered all her strength and stood up from the ground to demonstrate to him she was capable of lifting herself up, and she was not as meek as he probably had thought she was.

It was like showcasing who was the strongest between them. The sight switched on a light in Jenny's heart like an automatic switch. And Johnny's physique brought in sunlight to Jenny with beaming rays that almost blinded her eyes. She was mesmerised by how striking he was. Her world warmed up in seconds. And at that moment, she knew he was the man of her heart – tall and handsome. But it was too early to judge.

Jenny was unaware of what awaited her and knew she had to prove to Johnny, who ruled in her world. The new emperor made her heart smile, but she remained in control even though he was an exciting catch. Jenny was compelled to test him to see whether he would jump to her rescue if she fell. She wanted to make sure he was going to be a responsible man.

She walked towards him and pretended to fall. Quickly as lightning, Johnny stretched out his solid arms and caught her. She shoved him away and told him she was capable of supporting herself.

Johnny glared at Jenny and said, "You are a tough cookie. I like it." He told her he was willing to do whatever it took to get her.

Jenny, on the other hand, secretly thought his swift response demonstrated he had the potential to be thoughtful, reliable, and protective. She had perhaps found a man of her dreams – or so she thought.

Their courtship moved on quickly, and Johnny found out Jenny lived near the shanty area he had visited, but in a better environment than the slums, he'd witnessed. He soon learnt she had once lived in the wealthy gated community but had ended up in her situation after she'd lost her job. She'd remained unemployed for an extended period, and she had no family in the city.

Johnny told her he was interested in her, not where she came from. He asked her whether she would move with him to England. Jenny hesitated and asked him to stay in Kenya instead. Johnny insisted on going home because of his business, which he told her was demanding and required attention to detail. She asked him about the company as she wanted to learn more about it. However, Johnny disclosed nothing about it, but he assured Jenny they would be partners in the firm. She didn't want to pressure him, so they didn't talk about it.

Before long, their relationship moved a step further. Johnny would go to Jenny's flat, or she would go to his hotel. Finally, they agreed they were in love with each other, and they were ready to progress to the next level in their relationship. They soon moved in together in a new apartment, and their dating became official.

Johnny did whatever he could to please Jenny and served her every need. However, just when their love was gathering momentum, he realised his six-month visitor's visa was about to expire. Johnny didn't want to go back to England without Jenny, and she wanted him to stay in Kenya. He came up with a plan. But Johnny didn't know how to approach Jenny about it. He was afraid she would reject his idea because it was Jenny's way or no way. To get her to agree to things, he had to convince her it was the right thing to do.

Therefore, he decided to have a romantic picnic at Karura Forest to break the news of his intentions. He thought that bringing about the reminiscence of their first encounter at the forest was theright way of generating emotions.

He made the arrangement for the surprise discreetly because he knew Jenny didn't like surprises. He had to convince her to accompany him to the mystery venue. On their way, Jenny noticed they were heading towards Karura Forest but kept quiet. Johnny told her he wanted a quiet moment with her in the woods. Jenny loved going to the forest because of its serenity, so she didn't mind.

When they reached their destination, Johnny asked her to turn away from him and close her eyes. When he asked her to open her eyes and turn around, he had laid down the food on a colourful blanket, and there were two wine glasses and a bottle of champagne in a cooler. She smiled at him and said, "Oh, this is beautiful." She wrapped her arms around his neck as he fondly gazed into her eyes and told her he just wanted to make her happy.

They fed each other juicy strawberries as they spoke about their first encounter and their feelings for one another. They reminded each other how they'd both wanted to see the dominant one and laughed.

Finally, Johnny asked Jenny to pick a flower that was behind her. But Jenny stared at the flower and told Johnny she didn't want to ruin it for other people who may want to admire it. He then persuaded her to go to a bunch of similar flowers so that he could take a photograph of her. Slowly,Jenny walked towards the flowers, and all of a sudden, sparkle from the flowers shone straight into her eyes.

A Woman's World and the Men In-Between

The midday sun's rays shone directly on the flower, and Jenny was drawn nearer to it. When she looked closer, she discovered a diamond ring sitting correctly on the pink petals of one of the flowers. Jenny looked at Johnny, hoping to see a reaction, but there was nothing. She looked at the ring again and stared at him.

"What?" he asked her.

"You didn't do this?" she asked. "Do what?" Johnny replied.

Jenny bent over to look at the ring, and as she picked it up, Johnny took photographs. Then he walked towards her and wrapped his arms around her waist. He had a big smile on his face, and without a word, he went down on one knee as Jenny held the ring and said "Jenny, I would be honoured if you became my wife. Would you be my future queen?" Jenny looked at him with a smile. She paused, as Johnny's eyes remained glued on her without blinking. Finally, she shouted, "Yes!" I will be honoured to be a compromising wife, an equal, and a queen of our queendom."

Johnny didn't grasp what Jenny had implied with her answer as he took the ring off her and slid it onto her slender ring finger, gazing into her eyes. He was relieved she had accepted his proposal.

From then on, Johnny attended to all of Jenny's needs without a fuss and worshipped the ground she walked on. She was a goddess in his eyes, and he soon recognised his allure had sucked her right into his arms.

Likewise, Jenny was on cloud nine. She thought she had found someone to help her achieve her mission and believed the powers she needed to make her a success were intact. She was captivated by his effort to make her happy that assessing and scrutinising him before welcoming him to her life became secondary. The matter of the heart and body took control of her judgement, but she was ready to take the risk.

Jenny was always willing to deal with circumstances. Her painted claws were out. Her breasts were steady fast, and pointed like bullets, waiting for an order from the leader. Her legs were astride, and she stood with her arms akimbo. She felt like a warrior princess in her own right and a queen in her castle. She reckoned that, if Johnny thought they were going to be tied to the hip once they were married, he was seeking a bumpy ride.

She had vowed not to accompany him to England if he wasn't honest with her. Firstly, she wanted to know about his business. Secondly, she wanted to know about his family and where he lived. And thirdly, she wished to see if she would be able to get a job other than running the business.

He quickly cooked some lies because he didn't want anything to interfere with their relationship.

She told him she was a slave to no one, and the business should not be anything that could break her back. She said to him not to count on her to please him or worship him because no one was superior to her.

However, she was ready to find common ground within decision-making. Johnny assured her they would work together, and she would have an equal share of the business once she learnt the trade and the technical stuff. He told her he wanted to amaze her, and he had worked hard to get to his position.

Jenny supposed she had the brains, the hands, eyes, and other necessary parts of her body to do her job to the best of her ability. She was an independent woman who could do what she wanted and be whoever she wanted to be.

She desired to ruffle her feathers and fly. She promised herself not to let anybody stand in her way. She had all the armour she needed to fight her battle – a battle she was prepared to fight to the bitter end.

Jenny didn't care or feel threatened by Johnny's muscles, though they were eye candy and excited her and made her want to squeeze him close to her.

She craved his attention and the love that had been absent from her life, but she didn't want to be suffocated by him. Her freedom was paramount to her. And because she hadn't witnessed any flaws in Johnny, she concluded he was a 'modern man'. He cooked, cleaned, and opened the car door for her, and when they set eyes on each other, the attraction was magnetic. They were both spirited people, but her heart melted like a lit candle when she glanced at him. He complimented her and told her that she was a diamond sparkling on a dark night and that he was going to do anything possible to make sure her life was comfy.

Jenny fell deeper and deeper for his charm and attention. Her prince charming made her feel special, loved, and appreciated because of the way he gazed at her. She grasped that it was beautiful to have had such a catch. She had never believed there are such decent men left on earth. She considered herself lucky to have landed such a handsome man – a man of her choice and one she wanted to be with. She welcomed him into her life with open arms, and his love for her penetrated deeper into her heart.

She let her guard down, ready to ride his roller coaster ride and let him take her wherever he wanted. She felt lost under his wings. She imagined touching his six-pack and counting his muscles like waves in the Indian Ocean under the blue sky on the white sandy beach under a palm tree. His toned body was so fresh he looked like a god. When he embraced her, she felt as if he was a shield protecting her in the battle of love. There was nothing else she wanted in that department, apart from Johnny's attention.

She was a warrior princess who couldn't back down until she got what she wanted. The battle was nothing she had ever witnessed in the department of love. Johnny was the master. However, she was no slave. She had to own him too and give him a run for his money.

Jenny was ready to attack if attacked and willing to explore every opportunity. She was a fighter, not the average girl from the village.

She thought of how she had knocked out and hypnotised him with her eyes and beauty as he'd advanced towards her when they'd first met. She had blinded him with her attractiveness and pointed her two heavy bullets on her chest towards him. They were all natural with no bosom enhancers. He almost bashed over but managed to stay steadfast as his eyes focused on her voluptuous body. His pupils dilated, and Jenny could see her reflection in his piercing blue eyes.

At that time, all he could see was the figure of an angel in front of him as she swayed her curvaceous body in slow motion as if she was on a catwalk. She was ready to grind her gears like an armoured vehicle, and Johnny was immediately spellbound. She heard him say, "What a sight!"

Jenny's power was like a tornado, but Johnny didn't know how to respond to her advances. He thought that he had her figured out, but there was more to Jenny than met his eyes. Johnny hadn't anticipated that Jenny would be so tough. He'd expected her to be the one to follow him like a puppy. After all, that was what every woman he had been with had done. But Jenny stood there like she owned the world. She expected him to run around her and be honest about everything he did. She expected him to share everything equally, even the last biscuit in a packet.

Johnny assessed the situation, and he thought he had to establish her weak points before he could attack. Furthermore, he wondered what was in Jenny's thoughts because he couldn't get into her brain. Johnny didn't want regrets. He tried to do what he did best by using his power tools.

CHAPTER 18

The Smooth-Talker

Sweet talk softens the hardest heart.

Johnny used his mouth as his weapon to win the battle of love. He knew his kiss was smooth and delicate and melted in the ladies' mouth like Belgian chocolate. But every stroke was calculated, like the kiss Judas gave Jesus.

He made sure his voice went down Jenny's ears as if it was soft music. His touch was gentle, and his embrace was silky and warm. Jenny danced to his voice without music. And turned her to a puppet on a string with his shenanigans. It was what Johnny wanted. He was in control of her every movement, but she believed she was controlling him. Although she had seemed fierce when they'd first met, she had mellowed because of the attention he gave her to make her feel she was in control.

He seized the moment and played her the way he wanted. Now the relationship was intact, and he moulded her the way he desired. He turned her into an object of his desire buying her whatever she wanted – expensive clothes, handbags, jewellery, and the latest wigs and make-up.

However, he was wary of her. He had to be tactful and capture her capacity to have an influence on him. He was certain Jenny was not a mere woman. She was like a calm river that ran deep. She was fierce underneath all that beauty, and he was not gullible to let her fool him.

He knew the way to get Jenny under his control was to entice her. He flaunted his six-pack body in front of her after they had eaten a romantic meal in a hotel room and knocked her over. She couldn't take her eyes off him as she blew his trumpet and fell right to his feet.

She was demolished by his weapon of mass destruction. When Johnny gazed into her eyes, he smiled and realised he had seized her powers as he heard her whimper beneath his toned body. He listened to her heart, palpitate like an African drum against his chest, but she was not ready to make a complaint.

Jenny couldn't comprehend how a man could absorb her energy and make her feel weak. She considered that he may have some magic that confused her and turned her into something she didn't understand. His weapons made her feel high and sent her into a trance. She was catapulted to cloud nine. And as he whispered in her ear, she said in her heart, "Johnny, what are you doing to me!"?

She wondered how any woman could resist him with such a smooth voice. But some questions crossed her mind. With all his handsomeness, why was he not already taken by a woman? She didn't want to judge. But she didn't want to be fooled.

She wanted to remain on top.But Johnny had sucked her into his world with his stature and smooth talk. And she was infatuated by it all. Johnny made her high when she inhaled his breath. His breath penetrated her bloodstream and made her feel like she was on gas and air. Her encounters with him made her want the effect to last forever. If it did, their life would be picture-perfect.

Jenny admired his chest as it inflated and deflated and imagined laying her head on it as if it was a soft cushion for the rest of her life.

Teardrops ran down her face like pearls when he made her laugh. She couldn't repel his voice, and whenever he spoke, she imagined being in the Garden of Eden, just the two of them, like Adam and Eve. She was ready to share the apple with him at any time, but she remembered that she hardly knew him that well. Therefore, she decided to take her time. She would study him like a map, in case she got lost on her journey to the promised man.

Johnny pledged to protect her as if he were a commodore and never let her go. And he complimented her on how fit she was. Johnny knew his charms were the regulator. He was winning the battle of love and dominance.

Jenny, on the other hand, was not fooled by the compliments, as she was confident with her body. But she appreciated his effort, and she reminded herself not to forget her principles.

She finally decided there was nothing wrong in letting Johnny take the lead instead of fighting for dominance, as long as the control was shared equally. He respected her, and they did things together, and that was what she wanted. The sweet words from him – my diamond, my angel, baby, and honey – sounded like music in her ears. They were just words, but they made her smile.

She had never heard a man in her village use these words with their women or praise them. Therefore, she fell stupidly in love with him and let him take charge of her life. She believed he was different. In fact, she thought he was the most adorable male she had ever set her eyes on – a man she could work with to save womankind.

All this time, Johnny avoided disclosing too much about himself. He took his time and remained convincing. Every move was crucial, and that was what made him feel like a man with supremacy. He asked Jenny to trust him, as she was safe in his hands. Then again, she didn't want to be looked after. She wanted to be on the same page as him when it came to decision-making.

Jenny thought Johnny had a lovely nature. Therefore, she shared with him her village story. He told her he would be there for her, protect her, and promised never to hurt her, or make her cry. He whispered in her ear that he never wanted to see her eyes turn into a river running down her bright cheeks. He assured her his love for her would never run dry. Power and money were nothing to him. What he desired in his life was her love, and he would support her in her fight for women's liberation. Jenny weighed up what Johnny said. Is he for real? She wondered.

CHAPTER 19

Johnny the Lover

He captured her heart, locked it in, and discarded the keys.

Johnny's power and constant compliments and promises captured Jenny's heart and made her a prisoner of his adoration. She let him lock up her heart and throw away the keys without complaint. Jenny thought that he belonged to her, and she belonged to him.

His image was stuck in her brain forever. She had no worries. Johnny was her king, and she was the queen of his heart. His love for her had turned into toxic gas, and he was the one with the remedy.

She had never seen a man adore a woman like Johnny adored her. He had the shining armour, and he was ready to fight for her love and rescue her from loneliness. Thinking about his determination to secure her love for him, she felt she had found what every woman wants, a man to fight for her love. But as much as she adored him, Jenny wasn't prepared to surrender her rights.

Even though their love was sweeter than she had anticipated, there was a mystery about Johnny. He wouldn't disclose information about his business, and he didn't talk much about his family. To try and discover what he was about, she followed his shadows day and night, trying to catch him with something and analysing who he really was because she smelt some smoke.

In the process, he corrupted her mind, enticed her, and blinded her with lies. She was unable to see beyond his good looks. His swagger was like that of a lion in the jungle claiming his territory. He didn't want Jenny communicating with too many people or bringing them to the apartment. He told her he wanted to have quality time with her, and he closed off every chance of Jenny thinking otherwise.

Johnny had penetrated her mind, destroyed her medulla oblongata and dismantled the veins and nerves in her brain like the wires in a car and arranged them systematically the way he wanted them to be. He had used his tools to make sure that Jenny believed him, and he had given her no chance to doubt the information he passed on to her.

He intended to convince her to move with him to England. He knew that having a wife meant nobody would suspect him of what he was doing. Jenny was a novice in matters concerning love, and Johnny, with his enticing tactics, was able to access her secrets. But he was sure to tread with care, as Jenny's eyes were wide open.

Johnny thought Jenny was ready to grab any chance she had to assert her control. He knew a wrong move could have spelt danger, but he was confident he had put her under control.

However, when Jenny swayed her curves, his eyes were pulled towards her like a magnet. She was like a shooting star waiting to shoot across to him, and she was not afraid of falling. Jenny knew a parachute wasn't needed to catch her because Johnny was ready to. She also believed her life was in his safe hands. And their love for each other was as smooth as silk.

In Jenny's mind, she thought she had spun his head around 360 degrees and had him where she wanted him. He could not resist her, and the thought of it made her blood rise; her body temperature could have crumpled a thermometer.

Whenever she was with him, his touch was electrical. She felt as if she was on a bed of roses. The aroma from his body went through her nostrils and into her soul. It was clear she was caught up in his web. But she realised there are no roses without a thorn.

It was a dream for her to find a man who was her choice. Attractive, and who let her be in control of her destiny. However, she sensed her strength was ceasing the deeper she dug herself under Johnny's influence. But she convinced herself that their adoration for each other was mutual. They both thought they had dominance over each other, although only time could tell who would be the winner in the battle of their hearts' desires.

Jenny believed she was in dreamland when she was with Johnny. She enjoyed the attention he gave her just the way she liked it. His attentive care and gestures like opening the doors for her signified she was the queen. But on second thought, Jenny yearned to get into his head and extract everything in it and be in control.

She knew how to play the game and what would send him drooling and force him to vomit what was inside of him. She was ready to have him hooked like a fish on bait and make him salivate at the sight of her curves like a hungry dog in heat. She wanted to make him drink her like a milkshake, and she was ready to change to whatever flavour he desired, as long as she got what she wanted. She couldn't take her eyes off from him, but she was determined to go the extra mile to know everything about Johnny.

For his part, Johnny shook her like a maraca until he got the right rhythm to lure her into staying with him and never leaving. He turned her world around and made sure the twinkle in his eyes was what she wanted to see, to confirm they belonged to each other. For that reason, Jenny didn't care what the world felt about Johnny. Despite her friends telling her that she was moving too quickly with him, she was ready to travel the world with him.

She felt her paradise wasn't far away. They planned to go to the coast for a romantic break before they made further plans about their lives together.

At the coast, Jenny felt she was in paradise on earth. She lay on the white beach in Mombasa under a swaying palm tree, drinking coconut water through a straw and gazing out at the deep blue Indian Ocean. The fresh, sea breeze blew her hair, and she felt fresh and revitalised.

While she lay on Johnny's chest, Jenny felt she was where she belonged. Soon, they strolled along the beach, holding hands, and she couldn't believe her eyes that Johnny was holding her hand in public. Jenny had never seen a man hold a woman's hand in her village. To her, it was a dream, and she was ready to commit to him. She felt there was no need to compete with him for control, but she had to make sure that her strength was maintained.

At the time, he controlled every piece of her, emotionally, mentally, socially, and physically. He took charge of everything. Jenny found it impossible to resist him. There was no one else around, just the two of them.

But the sea was waiting to wash them ashore if things become too heated. Johnny was all she needed, and she was ready to give him what he desired. There was nothing to stop her.

Her interests meant nothing. Johnny was the boss, and she was Johnny's only queen in the universe. He fulfilled her desires. Johnny was as hot as fire and respected her, and there was a lucrative future business coming up. He had no problem with her getting a job and he had also promised to help her fight for what she believed in, so she thought there was nothing else she needed. It was a win situation, and she had it all in the bag. So, she thought.

Johnny, on the other hand, had drained her strength and destroyed her dominance, but she was unaware she was in total danger of losing herself. He quickly stole her capacity to take charge of her life by letting her do what she wanted and serving her hand and foot. But he knew she would soon be under his spell with a click of his fingers.

Her friends complained she had abandoned them since meeting Johnny and warned her about him. But she was blinded by his charms. Anyone talking about her man became her enemy. She thought they were jealous because Johnny adored her and worshipped the ground, she strutted her curvaceous figure on – that her friends envied her because, unlike their boyfriends, Johnny wanted to spend every minute with her.

Jenny was convinced he was the man for her. She could feel it in her bones. But she didn't want to leave the country without alerting her mother, even though she had not seen her for years. Her wish was to support her mother financially and to move her from the shackles of her culture. However, she knew if money were sent home, it would have made her mother's life miserable, as it would have caused tension between her mother and her father.

Therefore, she planned to sneak back to the village. Go to her local shop in disguise and leave a letter for her mother informing her that she was safe in the hands of her dream man – a man she had chosen and who loved her. She was sure her mother had had sleepless nights for years thinking about her, and she would have liked her mother to know where she was and to meet her future son-in-law. But she had to keep her location a secret. She had committed a crime by shaming her father and her family when she had run away from home. And now she was having an affair with a foreigner.

After two weeks, Jenny went back to the village and received reports from the shopkeeper that her mother wanted her to come back home. Her mother was also not convinced about Jenny's new man, and Jenny couldn't take her fiancé to the village. She knew he wouldn't be welcome, and she would have been the talk of the town.

Jenny was sure her father would not approve her choice of a partner or welcome him into the community. Furthermore, he was not ready to forgive her for dishonouring the family, and most of all, for making him lose the hefty bride price she would have brought.

She learnt that her father was like a dragon breathing fire when he heard that Jenny had been seen near the village. He blamed her for making him feel ashamed to participate in other men's dowry ceremonies for their daughters, as they always brought up the issue of her disappearance. The men accused him of not having a tight enough leash on Jenny, given that she had broken free.

Her mother told the shopkeeper to inform Jenny that she wanted what was best for her and to arrange to meet her. She didn't want Jenny to follow in her footsteps. And if the man she was with made her happy, that was all she wished for her.

Jenny was the first girl in the village to break the cycle of the cultural practices that oppressed women. Therefore, meeting up again with her mother was crucial.

Jenny arranged a secret meeting with her mother through the female shopkeeper, and when she met her mother, tears of joy poured freely from their eyes. Her mother squeezed her tight and told her she had a choice – she should do whatever made her happy and be wherever she wanted to be. But her mother warned Jenny to be careful and to do her homework and gather every information necessary about her new man before settling down with him. But Jenny told her mother she had nothing to worry about; she had Johnny figured out – or so she thought.

Linnet wanted to emphasise to Jenny that she shouldn't be fooled by a man's looks, sweet talk, wealth, or nationality; a man could change like a chameleon to get what he wants. Despite what her mother said to her, Jenny's eyes were blinded by Johnny. Johnny had told her that, in his country, traditions that are oppressive to women are never practised and females have the rights to do whatever they want. That was what Jenny wanted to hear, and she couldn't see anything wrong with him.

Before Jenny and her mother parted, they embraced each other, and it was hard to let go. Her mother emphasised to her to get into the relationship with her eyes wide open and not to let her desire to fight for women liberation dwindle. As they waved each other goodbye, tears trickled down their cheeks, not knowing when they would see each other again.

What Jenny didn't comprehend was that Johnny controlled her mind like a computer. She was only allowed to download what he wanted, and he told her what he believed she wanted to hear. Her family and friends were a distant memory, and that was how Johnny liked it. He wanted her to himself, and he told her that what was important was their happiness. Johnny told Jenny she had what she needed in the world. A man of her choice. A job, her independence, the time of her life and he was ready to support her in every way. As for him, he had money, power, and a beautiful woman.

After romancing Jenny for months, Johnny decided it was time to take their relationship to a different level. Johnny and Jenny tied the knot in a registry office in Nairobi with two strangers as their witness, and he didn't have to pay the dowry.

They then arranged to fly to England. Jenny felt it would be a fresh start, but she was bothered that Johnny hardly spoke to her about his aristocratic family. He changed the topic every time she mentioned his family.

Jenny loved Johnny, and she didn't want to seem as if she doubted him. However, although they had spent a significant amount of time in each other's company, sometimes she felt suffocated by his constant attention. Jenny put it down to his obsession with her and that he had too much love for her. She concluded that he was protective, and she believed him to be her soul mate. She felt she was going to know the real Johnny once they were in England.

Jenny had never had a passport before, and she found out, to get one quickly, she had to pay a bribe. She refused and threatened to report the matter to the authority, and as a result, she was given one very quickly. She obtained a spousal visa, and soon, she and Johnny were on their way to England.

CHAPTER 20

A New Life

The city of dreams.

Soon Jenny and Johnny landed at Heathrow Airport in England. It was seven in the morning in June, and Johnny smiled. However, when they came to the immigration booth, Jenny was asked to step aside, and her passport was taken. The immigration officer flicked through her passport while staring at her face and then questioned her, but he didn't seem to accept that she was Johnny's wife. The officer eyed her and then stared at the picture on her passport. Jenny was dressed in her Maasai traditional attire. After the officer was satisfied with his scrutiny of her, he told Jenny she had to go through further investigations. She was surprised to be told she had to go through a medical check-up. She asked why and she was told it was part of the immigration process, and she was led to a cubicle. She looked around, wondering what was happening; she wasn't ill.

When they got to the cubicle, she was asked if she had swallowed anything "Apart from food and water, no " she answered, aghast.

She had an X-ray done, and after sometimes, the officer came back with a smile and told her everything was okay. She received her passport back and was told she was free to go. She asked why she'd had to have the check-up, but Jenny was told she had nothing to worry about. She looked bewildered and wide-eyed and wanted to figure out what was happening as she walked to Johnny's side.

Still not knowing why she had been singled out, she asked Johnny why it had been only her who was pulled out and not him. He suggested that perhaps it was because she wore her traditional Maasai dress, and the officer may have assumed it was a cover-up for drug smuggling.

With a face like thunder, Jenny looked at the officers and shouted: "I carry drugs, never". A female officer told her not to worry; it was just a process it wasn't anything personal.

When they got to Johnny's mansion, she missed seeing people with big smiles. The distance from home and the fact that she was in a foreign land hit her, but she was happy she was away from her nosy friends and neighbours. It was a new beginning to her destiny with a man who loved and cared about her. She wanted one day to go back to the village and face her father and introduce her man to him.

Johnny told her she was free to do whatever she wanted with her life, and her first idea was to accustom herself with her surroundings and get a job. She was determined to work and provide for herself. She didn't want to rely on Johnny, even though he had boasted he had millions in the bank and said she didn't need to work for the rest of her life as long as they were together. Jenny was not convinced about that. She wanted to be financially stable. She refused to waste her life away by staying at home.

With time, she felt comfortable and secure in Johnny's presence and in her new environment. She trusted him. Therefore, she asked Johnny whether he would help her to liberate young girls from the bondage of being historically viewed as the weaker sex. She wanted to one day go back to her village, stand firm, and rescue the girls from the torturous cultural traditions they endured. She desired to take them somewhere safe, somewhere where they could reach their full potential through education and support and realise that they are not toys to be played with.

She also wanted to be the global spokesperson for the women who live under the shackles of power and control of the world's societal and governmental systems. She told Johnny women's voices should be heard and their rights respected. She considered herself to be with a man who gave her freedom. And that was what she wanted for all women. She wanted them to be able to speak their minds, do what they want, and achieve their goals without restrictions. She feared for women who are subjected to abuse, humiliation, and financial inequality.

Johnny listened to her without interrupting her.

When she finished talking, he told her the kind of men who do such things to women are sick, and they should be locked in cells, and their liberty restricted. He assured Jenny she was a woman of resistance, strong and courageous just the way he liked his women.

Jenny stared at him sternly without blinking, her hands placed on her hips. At that moment, Johnny realised he had underestimated her. He had thought he had figured her out and drained her strength, but he wasn't aware her powers were buried deep inside her, waiting to explode.

He was fearful of what more Jenny had up her sleeves. He concluded she wasn't an ideal candidate to help him run his business. Johnny told Jenny she had a dangerous kind of ideology, which wasn't right for his company. Jenny, on the other hand, wondered what Johnny meant by that statement and asked him to elaborate, but his reply was farfetched. He told her she was his first and only queen, and he would support her in whatever she wanted to do.

Jenny had her reservations. She refused to fall for his reply. Johnny hadn't introduced Jenny to his family or anyone, for that matter, apart from a few friends who he called business associates.

Jenny thought that getting a job would get her out of the house and increase her social circles. Maybe then Johnny would open up to her about his family.

She got a job in a company without a hassle and interacted with many of her work colleagues. Soon, her social circle increased, and she formed friendships with a couple of girls and men. She went out with them on Fridays. In the process, it transpired that she discovered one of her colleagues knew Johnny. This colleague issued a warning to Jenny about her husband; she told Jenny she shouldn't be with Johnny. But Jenny concluded that the woman was jealous of her picture-perfect life. She was not a close friend of Jenny's, not like the other girls she had befriended, and she had seen the woman smile at Johnny.

Johnny took Jenny out at lunchtime and picked her up from work. He was always driving different cars. One time, Jenny had seen the woman staring at them in the car park from the office window. She thought the woman fancied Johnny and wanted to cause a conflict between her and Johnny so she could get hold of him.

Jenny wondered why the woman was bothered about her relationship with Johnny. She was not interested in listening to her opinion about Johnny. Jenny considered her life with Johnny as the happiest ever and wasn't prepared to let anybody interfere with her relationship. Jenny reasoned that Johnny had never treated her wrong. He had always taken care of her and let her do whatever she wanted. So how could she listen to a single woman?

Jenny was excited to get a job, as Johnny had decided she couldn't take part in his business. He said it was a secret service company, and there was no need for a new worker. He assured her that, once the time was right, he would include her. But she was his wife, and she wanted to know more about the business, regardless of whether or not she was a staff member. Johnny's refusal to give her any information made her wonder what sort of activity he was running, and it gave her sleepless nights.

Her mind went wild with different thoughts about it. Then again, she was happy and wanted to concentrate on her job while Johnny focused on his. Nevertheless, she couldn't let go of the idea of getting a glimpse into Johnny's firm. Although Jenny didn't want to argue with him, she was not happy with herself for letting him break one of her ten principles – that they would not keep secrets from each other. She expected him to tell her everything. She didn't want gossip going around about him to affect their life together.

After four months of being together in England, Jenny realised Johnny's world was closed, and he stopped involving her in what he did. She thought it was to do with the nature of his job, and she was determined to work and take care of herself and be financially stable. She wanted to be an independent woman and be able to fulfil her desire to rescue girls from male bondage.

The thought of earning her own money excited her. She planned what she did with her salary. Johnny wasn't interested in what she made.

He bought her what she wanted, and money was not an issue. But she wanted to be in control of her life, and she didn't want Johnny to always buy her stuff. She was in no doubt that her husband was a gentleman. And he treated her like a queen. But she wanted more than that. She had a perfect life, but she felt she could only buy the clothes that Johnny liked, as he paid the bills.

Later, Johnny convinced Jenny to open a joint account, telling her it was essential to save money together for her security, just in case something happened to him. He gave her the freedom to spend the money in the account in any way she wanted for one month. What she was not aware of, however, was that it was just an illusion.

CHAPTER 21

The Tragic End of Jenny's Power

The only thing that attracted Johnny in Jenny's new image was her stilettos. They demonstrated power in every stride that she made around the house, but he knew it was just a matter of time before he broke her like the broken sole of a shoe.

Jenny's desire to transform the way she dressed felt no different from what most women would do when they get a white-collar job. She went on a shopping spree on her own without Johnny for the first time.

She bought shoes, executive clothes, handbags, and make-up. She had no warm winter clothes, so she stocked up on that. And she also bought some beautiful clothes for going out. She wanted to feel and look fabulous. Up until then, Johnny had chosen her clothes whenever they'd gone shopping, according to his taste, because he paid the bill. Jenny felt it was time for her to pick her own clothes.

She was aware of her well-proportioned figure, and she wanted to dress accordingly and walk majestically around the house, displaying her new stilettos and clothes for Johnny.

As she presented her new clothes like a peacock spreading its beautiful colourful wings, she could see Johnny's smile fade away at the corner of her eyes. He glanced at her in a way she had never seen him look at her before, and with a smile on her face, she asked him whether he liked her new appearance.

Instead of complimenting her, he told her he liked the stilettos but not the clothes or the make-up.

Jenny believed the clothes moulded to her shape, and she didn't have to rely on Johnny's opinion to make her feel right about the clothes. She decided to wear what she pleased and not what. Johnny dictated. If it felt great, that was what mattered. Therefore, she didn't consider Johnny's views or approval necessary.

She told Johnny her clothes were her choice. Johnny rushed to her, grabbed the shopping bags full of clothes she had purchased and hurled them at her face before storming outside with a face like thunder.

For the first time, Jenny felt she was seeing the real Johnny. Johnny had told her to be free and follow her desires. And here he was dictating what was right for her and okay for her to wear.

She realised he had been suffocating her with attention. But it wasn't about love. It was about control. He wasn't even happy that her friends invited her to go out on some Fridays. To her, these outings were a breath of fresh air away from him. She couldn't comprehend what the fuss was about as he also went out with his friends.

He wasn't keen on her going out without him, but he let her go with her friends as long as she didn't spend more money than he told her to.

Jenny told him she wasn't going out to spend money but to enjoy herself with her friends.

He regularly phoned her to enquire where she was or whether she was enjoying herself and what time he should expect her back home. If she were a few minutes late, he would be waiting for her, looking like a pressure cooker waiting to explode. His constant monitoring made it hard for her to enjoy herself. She felt as if she was on a leash at all times.

Every time she went out with her mates, Johnny told her to be careful with her women friends and not to get into anything she would regret. She never understood what he meant; she considered her friends mature and responsible.

Furthermore, she was an adult,and her life was her concern. She wondered whether her popularity with her work colleagues affected Johnny.

She always told him all about her work and friends, but his workplace and friends remained a secret. Besides, he was always on the phone, talking to his 'workmates. And she wasn't allowed to listen to his conversations. He locked himself in a room or went outside whenever he received a phone call. Jenny found it very odd to live with a man who she knew nothing about but who she also loved – someone she wasn't forced to be with. Being Johnny's wife was her choice.

Within months, Johnny told Jenny that she was going out too often while she should be at home with him snuggling on the settee with a pizza and watching his favourite movies. He told her she didn't need all the friends she had because the two of them should be there for each other, and that was what counted.

To compromise, Jenny cut down the amount of time she spent with her friends on weekends and reserved some weekends to be with Johnny at home. Yet, when he wanted to go out, he never hesitated. Nor did he tell her where he went, and he would stay away for long hours, at times spending nights away.

Johnny didn't like to be contacted by phone or questioned, but he expected Jenny to tell him where she went and with who. He gave her conditions and told her what time she was to be back home and regularly monitored her movements by ringing her.

Jenny got fed up with his monitoring of her social life. She felt they were becoming incompatible. Her intuition was that Johnny had become a big brother', watching her every move. She had given up her financial management by opening a joint account, but she wasn't prepared to give up her social life and her independence to please Johnny.

On one occasion, one of her friends at work invited her to a hen party. It was not something she wanted to miss, as she was one of the bridesmaids. When she told Johnny, he said to her she couldn't go, as he was going out with friends and wanted her to stay at home. She told him she didn't see anything wrong with them both going out with their buddies as she sashayed to the bathroom, immersed herself in a bubble bath, and then went into the bedroom to get ready for the evening.

She then dressed up in a red miniskirt and a white top, applied her make-up, and slipped into a pair of red stilettos, and she was ready for the party.

At seven o'clock in the evening, it was time for her to hit the road with her workmates. Johnny offered to give her a lift, but she refused. Instead, Jenny pulled out her phone from her handbag and called for a taxi. She expected to have a good time with her friends, and she had a big smile on her face.

Nevertheless, her thrill didn't last for long. Johnny came towards her with glaring eyes and a face that seemed like it was about to blow up. He demanded to know where the party was being held and how long it would last. She told him she couldn't tell him the place or the time because the girls had planned to go to different venues. He asked her whether they were going to the pubs. But she told him she wasn't the one who'd made the arrangements; the other girls had made plans.

Johnny didn't like her going to pubs without him, even though she didn't drink alcohol. He told her he wanted to protect her. But then, she remembered one Friday when she had gone to a local bar with him; Johnny had almost caused a fight with a stranger who sat opposite them. He'd accused the man of staring in her direction and had accused Jenny of flirting with the man.

Since then, whenever she went out with her friends, he ordered her to make sure that her phone was accessible at all times so that he could call her and make sure she was all right because he cared about her. But the way he spoke to her and the volume of his voice caused her to become conscious. Jenny felt Johnny was interfering with her freedom.

She became aware Johnny had pulled the wool over her eyes. She wondered why he was behaving so differently from the Johnny she had fallen in love with. He controlled her life and displayed her to his drinking friends like an ornament.

Before long, it clicked; she recalled what her work colleague had told her about him. Jenny wondered whether the woman was an ex-partner because she seemed to know a lot about him, but she had disclosed nothing to Jenny, apart from warning her to stay away from him.

Jenny became curious. She wanted to know more about what her workmate might have to say about Johnny. She was suspicious and felt uncomfortable being around the workmate and avoided her.

She regarded herself as a free spirit; it was her right to be where she wanted and to be with whom she wished. She thought of how she made sure she set aside time to be with Johnny, but it was never enough for him. He wanted to take her liberty out of her hands. He didn't see the need for her to have many friends or to go out with them. She quickly realised that whether in the East or the West, females suffer the fate of control and domination.

Jenny had thought that European men are civilised and educated on women's empowerment and freedom. She'd thought they don't follow the age-old tradition that viewed females as below the men when it comes to social factors and conditioned women to stay at home.

But she was wrong as no one knows a woman's experiences behind closed doors, and she suspected that underneath the smiles and happy personas of many women lay tormented souls. Their minds face an invisible danger of coercion and control that lurk around them like a bacteria, unseen by the naked eye.

With the realisation of what Johnny was trying to do, she planned to cut the bud before it grew further. She had to stop him fast. Stop him from infecting her with the deadly bug of being subjected to his pressure and submission. She considered herself an individual, and that was what she wanted Johnny to understand.

When the taxi pulled up outside the front door, Jenny strutted outside without looking behind her, leaving Johnny standing at the main entrance. She believed that his disapproval about her going out couldn't stop her. She walked toward the taxi, with the clicking of the stilettos echoing in the night air – click, click, click – and climbed into the cab, and waved at Johnny as the taxi drove off.

When she came back home from her night out at midnight, she found Johnny waiting for her at the door. She saw him scrutinise who was in the taxi. Two of her workmates were in the cab. He quickly went outside and asked them where they had been. The girls stared at each other, and one giggled and said, "the party."

Johnny asked the girlsfirmly where the party was, and they told him to stop being nosy and asked the taxi driver to drive off.

When Jenny and Johnny got into the house, the colour of his face changed to bright red. Jenny was tired, and she wanted to go straight to bed. However, Johnny demanded to know why she was late. He had asked her to be home by ten o'clock so that they could have some time together before going to bed.

Jenny knew Johnny was looking for an argument and refused to answer him. He asked her why her telephone was switched off. She apologised, but she didn't see the need to explain herself. He grabbed her hand and asked her to answer him. Jenny told Johnny that the phone battery had run out of charge. He asked her whether she had called or texted other people when she was away and before she could answer him, Johnny snatched the phone out of her hand and put it on the charger.

He immediately scrolled through all the phone numbers and messages that were on her phone. He enquired who the people who'd communicated with her on her phone were.

One particular male contact on Jenny's phone caught his attention. He wanted to know why Jenny had James's phone number and messages from him. He demanded to know who James was. James was Jenny's close friend, a man of few words. Johnny didn't like her having male friends. He had told her a man could never have a 'normal' relationship with a female without benefits involved. He glared at Jenny sternly and analysed her reaction. Jenny gazed into his eyes, and they seemed to be blazing with fire. The blue bedroom eyes were no more. His eyes had turned into marbles that were ready to pop out of their sockets.

Johnny accused Jenny of cheating on him with James. but She had no words for him. She stared at him, sternly and refused to justify herself. Her lack of response wound him up. He telephoned James on Jenny's phone and asked him what his business was with his wife. James seemed not to comprehend what was going on. Jenny heard James ask Johnny why he had called him late in the night.

Johnny clenched his fist and paced around the living room, biting his lower lip. He seemed not to get the reaction he had expected, and he shouted at James on the phone and forced Jenny to tell James never to contact her again and to delete her number. Johnny gave James a stern warning that, if he disobeyed him, he would pay the price and would live to regret his decision for the rest of his life because of what Johnny was going to do to him. James asked whether he was threatening him, and Johnny shouted, "Yes!"

Suddenly, Johnny deleted all the numbers in Jenny's phone and then smashed the phone against the wall in a fit of rage. Jenny imagined Johnny as a monster coming out of its closet. "What's wrong with you!?" she screamed at him. "Why are you acting all crazy!?" Am I not entitled to have male friends?"

She told him he had to buy her a new phone. He responded that she didn't need a phone; if anybody wanted to communicate with her, it would be through him. Johnny told her she wouldn't own a phone, and they would have a joint telephone if she needed one.

For the first time, Jenny was frightened of him. She couldn't comprehend where his aggression was coming from. The thought of them sharing a phone made Jenny feel like Johnny was slowly taking her liberty. She didn't like it. Johnny's private phone never left his pocket, apart from when he was using it or when he got his trousers washed.

Jenny screamed at him, disregarding his rules. She told him she was the boss of her life, and he was not going to control her or her communication with people.

Her refusal to share a phone made him walk straight to her face, stared into her eyes and told her she had no choice, and she shouldn't contact men or strangers.

Jenny vowed to get a new phone the following day. She purchased a new phone, one that was better than her previous phone.

Johnny hated to be challenged, and to demonstrate to Jenny, who was boss, he smashed her new phone into pieces. It was in that crucial moment that she recognised she was living with a monster who had hidden behind a caring and gentle demeanour. She was scared of him.

However, she was ready to battle and demonstrate she had a voice, and it wasn't going to be shut down. Her rebellion took Johnny by surprise. He'd thought she would crumble if he intimidated her. But here she was, swearing to buy a third phone.

Jenny was determined not to lie low and let him take control of her.

To Jenny's surprise, when she went to withdraw money from their account on a Friday morning, she found no money in their report.

Johnny had transferred the cash to his accounts. She was not aware he had different accounts and felt he had duped her into depositing her salary in the shared account.

Johnny decided Jenny was only going to have money to buy the essentials. Jenny was not keen on Johnny taking control of her finances. She questioned why he had withdrawn the money from their account without her knowledge and why she couldn't spend her hard-earned cash. Jenny demanded that he give her money back, saying she had the right to use it however she pleased, and she refused to live on a ration.

Johnny, without a word, dragged her to the cellar, pushed her in, and locked the door.

CHAPTER 22

The Flowers

The flowers didn't mean a thing.

When Johnny came back a few hours after locking Jenny in the basement, it was thundering, and lightning flashed outside the windows. As soon as he got into the house, torrential rains engulfed the land. He stomped straight to the basement and dragged Jenny to the living room without a word. She could smell alcohol on his breath.

Jenny was led up the stairs like a sheep to the slaughter, but she didn't shed a tear or beg him to stop. Her stance made him puff uncontrollably. She asked him why he was behaving aggressively towards her. For the first time in their relationship, he turned to her like lightning and – boom! – His fist landed on her face with a thud and catapulted her to the floor near the stairs.

A gush of blood splattered out of her mouth and nose. Johnny glared at her. "Never question me again!" he shouted.

She tasted the metallic-like taste in her mouth, but she was afraid to spit it out. She quietly gathered her strength and staggered to the bathroom, but Johnny screamed at her and punched and kicked everything in his way. Jenny couldn't comprehend how someone who had regularly declared his love for her could go from zero to 100 so quickly.

After a few minutes, Johnny followed her to the bathroom, and when she spotted him, she froze, thinking he was coming for a fight. Jenny was in a dilemma. Should she lock herself in the shower? Or should she let him do whatever he wanted?

Before she could make up her mind, he stormed in and apologised to her. He told her he cared about her and loved her so much, and he wasn't a wrong person.

He declared he didn't know what had come over him and made him do such a thing. He swore he had never laid a hand on a woman and asked Jenny to find it in her heart to forgive him. She felt his words go through her heart like a sword. She couldn't make herself look at him in the eye because her blood boiled with anger inside her. But she knew that, if she retaliated, she couldn't match her strength with his.

After the confrontation, Johnny told Jenny he would do anything she asked if she would bury the hatchet. Johnny grabbed the phone from his pocket and ordered something. By the end of the day, there was a knock at the door. Jenny was not allowed to answer the door. Within seconds, Johnny was back in the bedroom, holding something behind his back. He asked Jenny to forgive him and told her that he had a surprise for her. Jenny stared at him without a word. She could not believe he had bought her flowers after what he had done to her.

His brutality wasn't something Jenny had expected to experience. She knew women suffer cruelty from men, and it is something women in her village go through day in and day out, but she didn't foresee a similar act happen to her. She had asserted that no man would ever hit her, but here she was with a swollen lip, a black eye and spit that turned into blood but she retained her tears. She was determined not to give Johnny the satisfaction that he was weakening her.

The experience sent her heart racing with rage, and she felt her anger bubbling up inside her like a volcano. She then remembered that she was miles away from home, and that added to her frustration. She had thought she was living with an angel, but Johnny had turned into a devil.

Jenny had no one to turn to, as she had no phone and no immediate neighbour. What she didn't know was that Johnny was looking for a woman who was submissive to his authority and followed all his rules and regulations – not a headstrong woman who refused to follow his orders. Her stubbornness seemed to infuriate him. He felt that Jenny was testing his manhood, and he had to show her who was superior.

When Jenny left the bedroom, she saw Johnny's phone on the living room table. Johnny had gone to the bathroom. She grabbed it and called the police.

Within minutes, she heard a knock at the door, and Johnny came down the stairs running. When he looked at the table, he saw his phone had been moved from where he had left it and asked Jenny whether she had contacted the police. Jenny nodded her head. He warned if she said anything to the police, she would suffer.

Johnny answered the door and acted as if nothing had happened. He told the police he and his wife had had an argument and Jenny had stormed down the stairs and had fallen. Johnny stared at Jenny intensely when speaking to the police officers. Jenny told the officers that what Johnny was saying wasn't right and that he had punched her.

He later admitted to hitting her in the spur of the moment when they were arguing. He was asked to seek anger management courses to help him control his anger. He told the police that they would sort things out. Jenny demonstrated through body language that she was scared of him, but the police didn't read her communication and accepted Johnny's explanation of the event and walked out.

As soon as the police left, Johnny yelled at Jenny and told her that calling the cops was pointless. He said to her that she wasn't intelligent enough, and his choice of a partner wasn't a dominant, career-oriented, independent, argumentative, and demanding woman like her. He told her his ideal female was one who adhered to his orders and not a headstrong person.

He said to her that he never competed with women and that, if she wanted to try to fight with him, she could. But she would have to accept the consequences. He informed her that giving her a chance to do whatever she wanted was a way of monitoring her character and to inspect how much control she craved before pouncing and shutting her down for not acknowledging his power.

Therefore, he had to up his game.He was the lord of the manor and he had to show Jenny who the man in the house was. He gave her a stern warning if she called the police again, they would do nothing to him, and he would finish her off because he had influence.

Jenny wondered whether the judicial system was the same all over the world when it comes to female matters because here again, it was the voice of the male that seemed to be acknowledged. It appeared that what a man says has more power than what a woman says. Women's words are taken with a grain of salt, despite the evidence.

Johnny dictated to Jenny new sets of rules and restrictions. However, Jenny thought she could mould him into being the person she wanted him to be. Jenny had thought he would calm down and accept her as her own person and that she couldn't be tamed like a caged animal. She had stated that no man was ever going to suppress her life, or so she thought.

Her expectation of being equal to Johnny brought about the power struggle between the two, and now it fuelled the flames. Neither was ready to accept defeat or to bow to the other person. To assert his power, he reduced the allowance he gave Jenny from her salary each month. But Jenny refused to take the money, and as a result, he made a drastic measure. He decided that she didn't need the money anyway. Johnny controlled the shopping and refused to buy what Jenny needed. He decided he was not looking for a career woman but a woman who would be his ornament, a woman who would cook for him and clean up after him.

Jenny was too ashamed to talk to her colleagues about how Johnny had taken control of her finances. And also, what was going on in her personal life. She had defied the warning she was given by one of her work colleagues and paid the price.

Her friends were suspicious that her relationship was in turmoil. They thought her smile disappeared whenever Johnny came to pick her up from work, and she was always ready for overtime, while before, she couldn't wait to go home.

Jenny isolated herself from her friends, and her pride kept her a prisoner within herself. She refused to discuss her feelings with her friends. Jenny knew most of her work colleagues thought her life was perfect with a handsome partner, a good job, and a beautiful house. But her life was far from perfect.She had nothing to be proud of, apart from herself and her career.

Her independence was gone, and Johnny stopped her from going out alone. Whenever she wanted to go to the shop, they would go together. He shouted at her and called her names in public, and no one intervened, apart from staring at them. He emphasised that, whatever they did, they had to do it together. But it only applied to what he wanted to do.

Jenny kept quiet to avoid causing a scene. She was focused on the future, but she found herself looking down whenever she was with him, lest she is accused of flirting with men and called a slut. People stared at her when he made demeaning comments to humiliate her. She felt judged by the public, but Johnny walked majestically as if he owned the universe. She wished she could read the public's minds and see what other people thought when they saw her being embarrassed by him. She felt people were quick to judge without understanding her circumstances.

Johnny had hidden her passport and had told her that attempting to leave him would be a waste of time. He warned that, if she did try to go, he would catch up with her, as he had secret agents who trailed her every move. He told her that, if he couldn't have her, no other man would, saying she had become his property when they'd gotten married, even though he hadn't paid the bride price.

At work, Jenny's friends questioned why she'd suddenly stopped communicating with them when she was at home, but she wouldn't give them a clear answer. Rumours spread in her workplace that her marriage was in crisis, but she made every effort to conceal the facts about her relationship with Johnny.

However, at times, she felt like a bomb waiting to explode. Other times, she felt like an empty shell walking around. At work, she tried her best to smile even though her heart was bleeding. Despite the turmoil in her relationship, Jenny looked forward to her job as a solace to her battered ego.

Her work environment was her chance to be in a different location and away from Johnny. She had forgotten how it felt when they'd first met. She thought of all the sweet things he used to whisper in her ears before they had moved to the West. Now, the kind words had turned into threats and abuse. The thought of going back into the house ripped her heart into pieces.

Johnny had warned her that, if she discussed their marriage with anyone or contemplated leaving him, she would never see daylight again. She thought of reporting the matter to the police, but she had done it before, and she had been let down. She felt that without evidence, the police wouldn't arrest him for emotional abuse or threats; there was no visible evidence of these things.

She felt Johnny was destroying her from the inside out emotionally, mentally, and socially, and the police couldn't see her inner torment. She ascertained that reporting him would have turned into a situation of her words against his. Jenny felt helpless and unsafe and wondered who could protect her if the police couldn't. She had no one to turn to, and she thought that, if the cops here were similar to the ones in her country, she would create more problems for herself if she continued reporting him to the police and he wasn't charged.

One of her workmates had told her how her friend had called the police on various occasions during episodes of emotional abuse and death threats from her husband. But because there were no visible scars on her or evidence to implicate her partner in what she was reporting, the police did nothing, and the abuse intensified. Days later, the woman was finally murdered by her spouse. The story made Jenny understand how vulnerable she was, as Johnny was very manipulative and knew how to get his way.

Jenny pretended to engage in conversations with her friends when she was at work, but her mind was always calculating what she could do to free herself from Johnny's grip. However, she found no safe escape route. She had fears about the people Johnny was associated with, and she was even suspicious of her workmates, which made her feel intense.

She didn't know that love could be so sweet at one moment and so volatile the next. She glued a smile onto her face all the time to hide the torment she was enduring. She didn't know that money, her social life, and her yearning for independence was the pivotal point of their relationship that had turned Johnny into a stranger. Her husband was now a stranger she used to know, a man who wanted to take control of her entire life, while he was free to do whatever he wanted with his life.

Furthermore, she had no idea where he was getting his money from because his business remained a secret enterprise, and she was not allowed to use her money without his permission. Their relationship was one of one-way traffic.

He always made her believe she was at fault every time they had a disagreement. She couldn't do anything right. She avoided questioning him or arguing with him because it only escalated the situation. The abuse was something that Jenny had to put up with, and she hoped for it to end. Moreover, she couldn't discuss her ordeal with her friends because she felt as if all eyes were on her. She had ignored the warning signs about Johnny's character and her colleague's words of caution about him.

She was subjected to his authority, and she sensed their union may have been a sham all along. She considered that he may have had a hidden agenda from the beginning, but because of her inner strength and her desire to liberate womankind, he may have aborted his plan. It was evident to Jenny he had no real love; she believed that people don't hurt those they love.

Jenny felt reduced to an object that produced a commercial profit. She wondered what she had gotten herself into. Her family was a considerable distance awayand hadn't seen them for years, and Jenny had no way of communicating with them, especially her mother. She felt she had no support system around her. Johnny had cut her off from her social life. He was the only company she had when she was not at work and the only person who knew about her life. She was absorbed into his life, and she had no experience of her own. She had no legal rights to her life, her salary, her personal effects, or her liberty.

She worked, but she didn't enjoy the fruits of her labour. Her work colleagues had no idea what was going on in her personal life, and she avoided those who questioned her. Her smile masked the pain and the torment she was going through in the middle of a crisis.

Johnny took her to work and picked her up daily. Some of her workmates marvelled at how much Johnnyshowered her with love and affection; they told her she was a lucky girl. She had a man who adored her. Some wished they had a partner like Johnny. But what happened behind closed doors was top secret. He threatened her, saying that, if she set eyes on another man at work or discussed what happened between them with workmates, she would die, and so would all the people she engaged with.

Therefore, she kept quiet to protect herself and others.

The warning made her suspicious of the colleague who had warned her about him. She believed there was a traitor in her workplace.

Some of the girls seemed giggly whenever they were in Johnny's presence and played with their hair. Johnny, in turn, looked at the ladies and gave them winks, disrespecting her right in front of them. There were rumours that he had fallen for one of the girls, and the girl acted awkward whenever Jenny addressed the stories with her.

Many times, when Johnny spent a night away from home, the woman would look at her and smile. It made Jenny treats everyone with suspicion, and she avoided discussing her personal life. She was stuck in her shell, and she could not wriggle out.

Jenny didn't want to put people's lives in jeopardy, so she followed every command Johnny gave her and isolated herself and became a recluse. She thought that her husband cared about her, but he changed his colours like a chameleon to suit every situation. The only time Jenny could breathe was when she was away from home. But as soon as she went through her door, her life changed dramatically.

She had no time to herself or with her friends at work, and her communication with the outside world was cut off after she'd entered the house. She was fearful of Johnny and ashamed, and she believed that some of her women friends were judgemental. She worried that, if she were to disclose what was happening to her, they would wonder why she stayed in a toxic relationship.

She thought some of them had fake smiles, and she believed expressing her feelings to them would escalate the matter. They demonstrated contempt when things were all right between her and Johnny. She was afraid that, even if she had a discussion with her closest friend, Stephanie, Stephanie might share what she confided with the rest of the entourage. She was also worried that a traitor was lurking and would pass the information to Johnny.

She steadily gazed over her shouldersto see if she was being followed. She couldn't even trust her closest friends at work because Johnny told her he had informers within her company who trailed her every move. He swore that he would know whatever she did in his absence.

She thought there were secret cameras recordings her at the workplace and in the house. She believed any attempt she made to speak about anything would be captured, and Johnny would be alerted. To make matters worse, she had no knowledge of the sort of business he did, which frightened her. It intensified her fear and was careful of who to interact with. She felt everyone was a potential enemy, and the one person she'd put her trust in had betrayed her.

She knew the kind of girl Johnny had turned her into wasn't what she had aspired to become. She had been robust and fearless before meeting Johnny. Now, she wobbled like jelly whenever his name crossed her mind, as she didn't know what to expect once they got home.

He monitored her phone conversations, and she was not allowed to own a phone. She couldn't telephone people without him being aware of the call. He stood at her side every time she received a phone call and listened to her conversations. Johnnysaid to her he didn't want strangers contacting her. Neither were her friends allowed to enter the house. He told her he was protecting her from sick people, but Jenny knew better. She was not a fool. It was about controlling her. He knew that, by separating her from her social network, he was able to assert his dominance the way he wanted.

CHAPTER 23

The Fallen Warrior Princess

She couldn't match his strength.

During a conversation with her best friend, Stephanie, Jenny saw that Johnny stayed close, listening to every word coming from her mouth and checked her reaction to the chat. He knew Jenny had previously arranged a night out with her friends on Fridays, but he had stopped her from going out, and he wondered why her friend rang. Stephanie could only contact Jenny through Johnny's phone, and Jenny had to shout the caller's names whenever she answered the phone to make Johnny aware of the caller.

On this occasion, she failed to shout Stephanie's name, and Johnny ordered her to put the speaker on so that he could listen to the conversation.

At that moment, Jenny wished and hoped that Stephanie didn't mention anything that would provoke Johnny as he intensely watched her.

However, Jenny's twist of the tongue while in conversation with Stephanie made her address Stephanie by her colleague's name, Steve, instead of Steph. Stephanie laughed and told Jenny she may have been dreaming of Steve to call her by his name or suggested she must have a crush on their colleague Steve.

Immediately, Jenny's heart dropped as Johnny stared at her sternly. Johnny instantly screamed at her to switch the phone off and demanded to know why she engaged with other men after he had instructed her never to have male friends. Before Jenny could open her mouth to respond, Johnny rushed at her and punched her in the face and hell broke loose.

He grabbed her by her short hair, which was barely there, as he had instructed her not to have long hair or add extensions. Johnny was convinced that, if she did anything with her hair, she was doing it to attract other men.

He pushed her to the floor like a scorned man, stepping on her chest repeatedly. He accused her of defying his orders and disrespecting him by cheating on him.

Jenny grabbed Johnny's legs and tried to bring him down, but he repeatedly kicked her while she was still on the floor and had to let go. He vowed that Jenny was never going to see or speak to James or Steve again. Jenny retained her cool because she didn't want to give him the satisfaction of knowing that his restriction was destroying her.

Her calmness seemed to agitate him further. He wanted a reaction from her so that he could watch her crumble. Nevertheless, Jenny remained steady, looking directly into his eyes without a word, as if nothing had happened. Her reaction enraged him. He ferociously punched and kicked her all over her body and then grabbed her and tore her clothes.

Jenny screamed at him and asked him to stop violating her modesty. The next minute, she felt his hands squeeze her neck until her eyeballs rolled inside the sockets. He picked up a kitchen knife "I will kill you, and no one will know you are dead!" He shouted.

Within seconds he punched her in the face and cut her on the arms and legs. She was soaked in blood, lying on the white kitchen floor. Jenny knew that she couldn't fight him as she couldn't match his physical strength. Therefore, she pretended to be lifeless to save herself; it was all she could think about to have a chance at pulling herself back from the brink of death.

Jenny had thought she could conquer the world, and she could do whatever she wanted. She'd imagined that she could rescue womankind. Now, Jenny felt her intentions were fading fast. Here she was, powerless in Johnny's hands, like a piece of broken glass. She had demonstrated to him that lifting herself up from the ground wasn't an issue when they had first met, and now she lay on the cold surface, hurting and helpless. She felt like nothing more than a rag doll and a punching bag for Johnny. Her trust in him as her anchor became her downfall.

Having asserted his power over Jenny, Johnny stood up and lit a cigarette. He smoked standing over her body and turned her into an ashtray. She felt the heat from the cigarette ashes drop on her bloody, exposed frame. She couldn't do anything, apart from close her eyes tightly.

Despite the agony, she was determined to stay alive. She knew she had no escape process, and shouting was not going to help, as the mansion they lived in stood alone. She also didn't want to give Johnny the satisfaction of knowing he was breaking her emotionally and physically. She hoped to succeed in wriggling herself from his grip.

141

Jenny felt like a volcano waiting to erupt, but she had to wait for the right moment.

When she could no longer feel the ashes dropping on her body, and the silence filled the kitchen, she slowly opened her bloodshot eyes and found Johnny still standing over her head. He stood motionless thinking that she was on her last leg. There was not a single movement and not a sound for a long time.

When he saw that her eyes were open, he apologised for what he had done to her. As he spoke to Jenny, tears rolled down his cheeks, and he declared his everlasting love for her as he cuddled her tightly. At the same time, he blamed her, saying that it was her fault – that she had made him snap and hurt her. He accused her of pushing him to the limit by mentioning Steve's name. He told her that she had apparently formed a friendship with men behind his back to disrespecting him. But Jenny knew he had calculated the act in his head.

Jenny had no energy to argue with Johnny or to apologise, as she had done nothing wrong. He promised her never to hurt her again and asked for her forgiveness. He also made an oath with her blood. She agreed to forgive him for avoiding more blows, but she knew how much she loathed him.

Before she nursed her wounds, Johnny demanded to be intimate with her, despite her battered body. She had no strength to fight him or resist his advances and let him do what he wanted. Jenny stared at the ceiling and focussed her mind on something else so that she could forget the torture and block the aches in her body, but Johnny forced her to face him.

After her ordeal, she told him it was better they separated to give each other space and a chance to reflect on things and reconnect again. However, consulting him about a breakup was the worst mistake she made in her quest to escape. He informed her they would separate from each other over his dead body.

From that point on, Jenny knew she was in great danger. In her head, she figured out that, if he agreed to separate, there was no way they were going to be back together. But it seemed Johnny had read her mind.

She grasped there was so much she didn't know about Johnny and that she had jumped into the relationship blindly without getting to know his background. He had been subtle, to begin with. So, Jenny hadn't suspected what was happening. She had thought he had pure love for her, as he'd attended to her every need.

However, he had never introduced her to his family in the two years she was in England. He refused to discuss anything to do with his personal life. Johnny justified his failure to introduce her to his family with the fact that he hadn't met her family in Kenya. All Jenny knew about him was that he had a lucrative business, which she had never witnessed, and that he was an only child from a wealthy family who were farmers.

Nonetheless, Jenny had noticed he was always receiving many phone calls, which he would never answer in her presence. Whenever someone called, he locked himself in the basement. The basement was soundproof, so no matter how hard Jenny tried to listen to the conversation, she heard nothing. Jenny wanted to know what was going on. But Johnny informed her he was working on a high-profile job, and he had taken an oath not to discuss his role with people outside the company.

Johnny didn't expect Jenny to go to work for days, but to his surprise, Jenny woke up on the following Monday, ready to go to work. He knew she was too bruised, and she would alarm her colleagues. Her eyes were like a panda, and her body had turned black and blue. Johnny told her she didn't need to go to work. He was capable of providing for her. But Jenny argued that she could take care of herself.

He asked her to contact her workplace and ask for sick leave, but Jenny refused and insisted she had to go to work. Her failure to listen to him made him bar her from answering the door. Even if her friends or anyone else came to check on her.

Three days later, Stephanie came around to check on her, but Jenny was dragged to the basement so she couldn't shout. Johnny had watched Stephanie pull her car into the driveway, and before Jenny knew what was happening, she was locked in the basement. She felt like an animal in captivity, locked in a cage.

She knew dark clouds had fallen on her, but her life wasn't finished yet. Then again, she was afraid of never fixing her eyes on the bright blue sky, and she wondered whether she was going to come out of the ordeal alive. Johnny's eyes terrified her. He looked as if he was always ready to pounce on her. It was the first time she knew how it felt for a woman to be terrified by a man's presence.

While she remained determined not to be broken, Johnny's increasing infliction of fear made her dread she was losing the battle. She clung on to the hope that she could break free and that the summer sunshine would shine on her once more as she smelled roses. Jenny didn't believe she could be hidden away forever. Though giving up wasn't far from the back of her mind, but she remained firm.

The phone calls ceased, as Johnny cut her off from every means of outside communication. The outside world was closed to her. He took away the only freedom she had left. However, she still believed there was a small chance of escape and kept looking for it. However, he made sure the doors remained locked at all times, and the keys stayed in his pocket day in and day out. Whenever he ventured outside, he dragged her to the basement and locked her in the darkness. He had disconnected the electricity in the basement.

Jenny believed the mental torture was worse than physical abuse. She knew there would be no family out there worrying about her. Therefore, Johnny was free to do whatever he wanted with her life without people worrying about her.

To make this clear, he cut Jenny's clothes into pieces and told her she didn't need any clothes because she would never flaunt her body to the world ever again. Not only did he take her dignity away, but also her self-worth too. But Jenny vowed there was no way she was going to let him topple over her inner strength. She was ready to see the end to it all, and she trusted that, as long as she was alive, she would one day free herself.

Johnny went out to work most days and left Jenny locked in the basement for long hours without food. Whenever she questioned him about why he was torturing her, he refused to answer her, and if she persisted in getting a response, he became violent.

Stephanie continuously came to Jenny's house to check on her, but nobody answered the door. Finally, Johnny had enough. He asked Jenny to contact her workplace and all her friends using an unknown phone number. She was to tell the work colleagues she had gone back to Kenya on an urgent matter and that she was not coming back anytime soon. Johnny gave her strict instructions not to alarm friends and workmates.

He told her if she changed her tone of voice while speaking to her friends or scared them in any way that would be the end of her life.

When Jenny told her colleagues, she had gone back to Kenya, and that she was not coming back anytime soon, they couldn't imagine her leaving without contacting one of them. Stephanie asked Jenny whether it was for real, and Jenny answered with a trembling voice, "Yes." But still, she failed to respond to the rest of Stephanie's questions.

Stephanie's suspicion made her feel uneasy, and she reported the matter to the police. Johnny was queried by the police concerning Jenny's whereabouts, and the police were satisfied with his version of events. He told the cops that Jenny had gone to Kenya because her mother was terminally ill. However, Stephanie was still not convinced, but she had no way of getting further information about Jenny apart from Johnny who refused to talk to her and asked her to keep away from his relationship with Jenny.

Jenny had hidden what happened in her marriage. She'd always had a plastered smile on her face. In spite of this, Stephanie had seen through the smile. She knew that for a time before Jenny's disappearance, Jenny had not been herself. Whenever she'd asked Jenny whether she was all right, Jenny had avoided eye contact, and she seemed frightened of Johnny.

After being forced to lie to her friends, Jenny wondered what Johnny was planning to do to her. She pleaded with him to let her work to help her mother at home, but Johnny told her she would never see or contact her family again and that she was his property now, and she shouldn't have thought about the family. After all, she had run away from them, and no one would be searching for her.

He told her that her job had caused friction between them. Therefore, she was never going to work again. Jenny agreed not to work but pleaded with him to set her free from the basement. He didn't heed her request. Johnny left her housebound 24/7 in the cellar. When she was underground, she never knew when he was around in the house or when she was going to have her next meal. She was afraid to make the slightest noise or ask for food in case she angered him.

When he went to his secret job, he would set surveillance around the house to monitor her movements in the basement. He sometimes pretended to leave and appeared a short time later to scare her and to condition her that, even in his absence, he could reveal himself as a ghost. Jenny was conditioned to stay where she was in case Johnny was lurking within. She blankly stared at the walls envisioning terror unfold in her head that she thought she was losing her mind.

As the days went by, Johnny's attitude and behaviour changed. He seemed to have no self-control. It was his way or no way. Jenny realised

Johnny was erratic at times when he was under the influence of something, but she was not aware of what it was.

Out of frustration, she shouted at him that what people had said about him was right – that she had turned a deaf ear to their warnings because she loved him and had thought their union was a fairy tale. She said her colleagues had once been jealous of her picture-perfect life but later became fearful things were falling apart in her relationship. She told him they knew he was a devil and that was why they had tried to help her, but she had been blinded by his spell and had refused to listen to them. If she had, she would not be in the situation she found herself in now.

With those remarks, Johnny demanded to know who she'd had a discussion with about him. Jenny refused to reveal which friends had talked about him, and as a result, she was beaten to a pulp and left fighting for her life. She groaned in pain, and she was in and out of consciousness. After regaining consciousness, she begged him to take her to the hospital. He refused to respond to her plea and left without a word. She remained for hours locked in the basement with no light, lying on the cold concrete.

Jenny wished the earth could swallow her, but she knew, if that happened, Johnny would have won. She was never going to let him win whatever happened unless she died. Jenny was determined to demonstrate to him that he could break her physically, but he couldn't tear her inner strength. She fought to remain mentally and emotionally intact.

CHAPTER 24

The Keys

The keys in his hand.

Jenny thought she'd had the keys to unlock her potential. But keeping the keys tightly in her hands became an issue when she gave her heart to Johnny. Once he took the full control of her life, her capacity became limited. Her success was just a dream, as he had locked away her every opportunity to grow as an individual. Her future development depended on his mercy, but she never settled for defeat. She continued fighting to reclaim the keys to her future and unlock the door to her restricted life – the door that would take her to freedom. However, the more she fought, the more the bolts to the door were tightened, and she was left with no escape route.

Jenny was left in the basement in darkness for hours. When Johnny opened the door, he went straight to her and held her in his arms. Her entire body was sore, she tossed and moaned on the floor. Johnny told her she was his girl and his only remedy, and he needed tender loving care from his princess. He warned her never to break his heart. Jenny thought Johnny was insane. She couldn't believe how heartless it was for him to say such words to her after what he had done.

She found it hard to look at his face, but Johnny continued to tell her she was the most beautiful woman in the world and that she was lucky to have him. He said to her she shouldn't worry about a thing because he was there to hold her hand and provide for her, and everything was within her reach if only her behaviour didn't make him feel less of a man.

He told her she'd had it all, but she had thrown it away because of her stubbornness and disobedience. He said to her he was the only remedy for her. She should not have gone out in search of more from other men. Her destiny was with him and no one else.

In the middle of the conversation, he removed something from his pocket and asked Jenny to take it to ease her pain. Jenny demanded to know what it was, but he refused to tell her. Jenny declined to take the substance. Her entire body was on fire, but she didn't want to drink something without knowing what it was.

Johnny continued trying to persuade her to take just a bit, but Jenny only stared at him. Her refusal to accept what he was offering to her led him to force her to drink it, and she choked in the process.

Johnny told her that no one should say to her any different – she was his baby, and making her better was his priority. He whispered in her ear that people didn't want to see her happy, especially her work colleagues, like Stephanie, and she was a fool to believe what they had said about him.

From there on, Johnny brought a concoction of liquids to the basement every day for her to drink.He refused to give her food unless she had some. Jenny had to choose between life and death. She became alcohol dependent, and she couldn't do without it. Jenny had dark circles beneath her eyes and the colour drained from her face. Moreover, she looked like a stickbecause Johnny only gave her enough food to keep her alive.

For months, she was subjected to cruelty as punishment for not doing what Johnny wanted her to do. He denied her food and the substances he had gotten her addicted to, and he watched her writhe in agony. She felt butterflies in the stomach and suffered fits during which sweat drizzled profusely down her body, and her entire frame shook like an earthquake. At times, she felt ants crawlall over her physique. She believed Johnny was poisoning her with something because she had a feeling,she was losing her mind without the substance.

She had watery bowel movements, and her nose ran like a tap. Her skin was full of huge pimples covered by scabs and seemed infected. She picked on the spots, but there was no comfort. Every time Johnny denied her the substances; she was like a dead woman walking. She couldn't function without it.

Johnny tormented her by telling her she didn't know what tomorrow would bring, and if she were not a good girl, he would not provide her with the treats she desired. He stared at her sternly as his lips pulled up in a wicked, devilish smirk that always caused a chill down her spine and shouted at her and told her that it is a man's world, and a woman will never have a say because whatever a man wants, he gets it. That included Jenny's life because he was her god.

He told her she was living in paradise and she should be grateful. But to Jenny, she was living in hell on earth. She couldn't stop herself from craving for alcohol because of the effect it had on her health when she didn't take it. She had muscle pain, the sweat poured off her, she had Goosebumps,and she was a night owl without it. She begged him to give her some so that she could stop the effects. But he refused and only offered it when she was on the brink of death. Jenny was convinced that Johnny was giving her something else than just alcohol.

Jenny knew she needed medical attention, but Johnny ignored her. He rewrote their story, saying he had searched far and wide for many years for his princess. Johnny had finally met her, and they had both been happy, but she had turned out to be somebody else – someone Johnny failed to recognise. He told her that, despite everything he did to her, she should never have forgotten that his love for her was forever. Only death would separate them.

Jenny thought Johnny was irrational and a coward. She had no love for him. Their passion had faded when he'd hit her and took control of her life, and it had died when he'd subjected her to degrading treatment. However, it wasn't buried yet because he continued to have authority over her, and there was no escape. The time when they had met was in her past.She wanted to focus on her rescue mission and seek for her freedom and independence.

CHAPTER 25

The Game Player

The poker games.

Jenny felt Johnny played her like a game of poker and gambled with her life. He pretended to be kind to her, and then abused her. She surrendered her self-worth and dignity to him, knowing that was the only way to gain peace and liberty. She had once thought she was the queen of his heart, but he had taken everything she had. He hooked her onto a leash and released her from the basement when it suited him, but only under his watchful eyes.

He changed everything Jenny knew about herself as a woman. She realised it didn't matter how strong-minded a woman was; once she let a man take control, it was hard to claim her status back from him.

When Johnny recognised how bruised Jenny was and saw how, even though he had stripped her liberty completely, he had failed to break her spirit, he decided it was imperative to seek other means to torment her. He invited other women to the house. But Jenny demonstrated no signs of jealousy; her heart was not in the relationship. Jenny had made her decision. Johnny was not a keeper. If only he let her step out of the door, she would run away from him and keep running as far as her aching legs could carry her.

Johnny played a game of hide-and-seek with Jenny; she never knew when to expect him. He brought different women to the house and entertained them for a while before he subjected them to torturous acts of bondage. Jenny was made to observe his deed in the basement, but the women were unaware she was there. She wanted to scream and tell the women to run for their lives before it was too late. But it would have been pointless, as no one could hear her. Johnny always played loud music when he was with the women.

Jenny felt there were many tricks up Johnny's sleeves.

He played the blame game on Jenny, saying it was her fault that he brought women into the house; it was her lack of taking care of herself and her lack of interest in him that made him do it. He teased her in the basement by calling her sweet cherry pie and then went back to the women.

His manoeuvres were sleek and smooth. The females were not able to control themselves and resist his moves, just as she had been unable to resist him when they'd first met. They were not aware that she was hidden in the underground, watching as they were exposed to his manipulation and feeling helpless to rescue them. They kept on coming back to him – until they disappeared.

Jenny wondered what might have happened to the women. She hoped they had discovered Johnny was a wolf in sheep's skin and had run for their lives. The women seemed to have fallen under his spell, just like she had done long ago, and his game of love was the only game she knew how to play.

But the game of love had turned sour. He told her that, if she were somewhere else, she would be forced to cover herself head to toe to look like a ninja. He said she would be like a lump of clay waiting to be moulded into different shapes for lack of direction and the power to say no.

Jenny knew she had an opinion of her own, but Johnny ignored anything she said. She ended up not having her voice heard. Whenever Jenny opened her mouth, there was a forced smile on her face, one designed to make Johnny happy to save herself from more beatings. Her life revolved around him, and he told her that, without him, she was nothing.

She played his game to the maximum to stop him from torturing her; she knew he got a buzz from seeing her helpless and considered himself the stallion. But she believed that, if he genuinely were a stallion, he wouldn't have locked her in. He would have set her free and fought with her when she was at liberty. Locking her in demonstrated he was afraid of her, as she was capable of bringing his empire down and leaving it in ruins – if she found a way to escape his grasp.

She considered him a small man for subjecting her to torture and weak in mind and soul for mistreating her when she was restrained. She didn't find him the majestic king or Johnny the great. Instead, she saw him as a weakling. A man who had locked her in seclusion.Away from the world to assert his power and hide his insecurities. He had made her world insignificant and small, reducing it to four walls day and night.

Jenny thought of how her life had suddenly changed.

She had been living a fairy tale, and now she was living with a monster. The faces of women who harbour dark secrets that happen behind closed doors filled her mind.

She thought of the skeletons in the cupboard that have ravaged women's existence and how some women are too afraid to share what is happening to them. Others believe their suffering and torture is the norm or their fault; too many ladies may have taken these top-secrets to their graves because they thought they had to persevere with the hardship and the misery. For many, their mouths are shut through fear of the unknown, manipulation, and dominance.

The butterflies Jenny felt in her stomach when she and Johnny fell in love had now turned to a cold chill when Johnny was near her. She couldn't look at him directly without being accused of having no respect for him. The bed of roses was thornier than she had expected. The honeymoon was a thing of the past. She lived in a torture chamber but would her ordeal ever end?

CHAPTER 26

The Goal Shooter

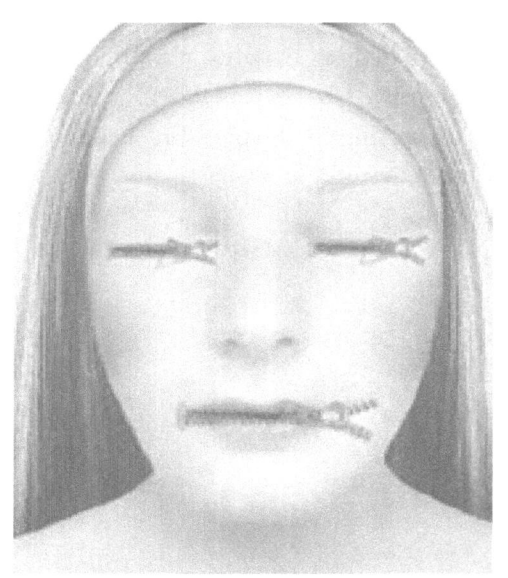

Silenced

Once Johnny was sure Jenny was unbreakable mentally, he thought there were no more challenges, and that meant there was no fun. There was no need to hang around if he couldn't cause fear in her life. Jenny had become numb to the pain, and his treatment didn't seem to have much effect on her. She refused to pretend that things were all right. Johnny devised more torturous procedures to force her to acknowledge his presence. But she remained unmoved.

He searched for other challenges to thrill him and found different ways of quenching his hunger for power and control. Johnny brought various women into the house, accompanied by men when he realised, he couldn't mould Jenny into what he wanted her to be.

Although her mouth was sealed, she was not blind. She could see what was going on in the house. Jenny observed the activities in the house from the basement through the CCTV that Johnny had installed. She remained a spectator in her confinement while hours faded away.

Even though the cellar was soundproof, Johnny warned Jenny not to cough or make the slightest noise when she was in the basement while the women were around. Other men were invited to use and abuse women. It tore Jenny's heart in pieces seeing the women so vulnerable and being exploited and subjected to degrading ordeals.

Her life was no different really, and she found it hard to judge the women, in terms of why they didn't run away. She had been in their situation once, but she hadn't managed to escape. The women seemed to come from all nationalities, and their every move was scrutinised. They were led like sheep and forced to act as if they enjoyed what was happening and danced erotically wearing skimpy lingerie's, but she knew what was happening to them was against their will.

One of the girls seemed to look directly into the camera unknowingly, and Jenny could see the sadness in her eyes. The girls seemed to smile with their eyes and cry with their hearts. Jenny realised that brutality against girls and women is a global epidemic. And those with the power to protect them contribute to it, as they do little or nothing to safeguard the victims' lives, well-being, and their future.

Jenny thought about the women left with no hope of ever living their lives freely. She felt that, unless women fight for their rights, they are likely to be shut down by those in authority and remain in modern-day slavery, waiting for another William Wilberforce to come to their rescue.

As Jenny witnessed the girls' ordeal, Rosie's story came flooding into her mind. She wondered whether these girls had fallen prey to human trafficking after being lured with a promise of an opportunity for a bright future. Their smiles plastered on their faces told a different story. They came to the house during the night, followed by different men.

Jenny knew she had to play Johnny's game to the letter if she was ever going to come out of the darkness alive. But she refused to keep quiet. Jenny questioned him about what was going on, asking him what business the men coming to the house had with all the girls ferried there. She was sure she had discovered his secret life – the one he had tried to hide from her. The women were his business. No wonder he often received numerous phone calls that he wouldn't answer in her presence, claiming the calls were about business matters.

He never disclosed the sort of business he did or where he was working. Jenny knew what was going on. Johnny tried to convince her it was all in her mind and that what she had seen were visions from Rosie's story. Then again, Jenny was aware of what was witnessed; and wasn't losing her mind. She recognised there were many Rosie's around the globe, waiting to be rescued. But who would save them?

Jenny wanted an answer from Johnny, but he tried to play with her mind. He told her she was paranoid and going crazy, even with the evidence that she was forced to watch. Playing with her thoughts, the idea of making her psychologically disturbed gave him satisfaction. But Jenny was much more focused, and she knew herself better than Johnny knew her.

She was sure there was nothing wrong with her mind.

Nevertheless, eventually, she had to accept everything Johnny said to her, and she told him he was right; she was the crazy one. She did this to her advantage. She knew that to find an escape route, she had to pretend Johnny was right about everything. It was a game Johnny played, and Jenny had to participate. It was all part of her plan to free herself. She was confident the girls were being trafficked, brainwashed, and controlled, just like Rosie had been. She knew she was their only hope, so she had to play it right.

The sort of treatment Jenny received and watching the girls' sad faces made her believe girls will never be safe in the world if nothing is done to stop the brutality and mental torture. They are vulnerable in the presence of men, regardless of their status.

Jenny couldn't believe such a thing happened in a developed country under the noses of the community and the authority. She wondered how many other women are locked in and their mouths zipped shut.

The girls were transported at night and seemed not to chat with each other when they were in the house. From the basement, Jenny viewed everything that was happening in the rooms. She saw the girls being forced to consume substances – either by drinking or smoking them – before they engaged in their acts, and they seemed compelled to perform.

Jenny tried to investigate what was going on by asking Johnny, but she received more beatings every time she questioned him. He told her she was paranoid, and he didn't know what she was talking about. But she knew Johnny was the one with the problem, not her. He was the one who was insecure and controlling her. Johnny used his power to manipulate her because of his weakness. She felt if Johnny were a macho man, he wouldn't have made her his slave. And it wouldn't have been hard for her to release herself from his shackles – if only she were not a prisoner in his cellar.

Jenny's effort to do whatever Johnny asked to turn things around was met with aggression. She felt he had forgotten where they had come from. Jenny had thought they were unbreakable when he'd held her tightly during the good times. She had told him everything about herself because she had trusted him. Now, she was merely hanging on by a thread.

She remembered her mother's words of advice before she had left home; her mother had told her to be cautious and make her choices wisely with her eyes wide open. But Jenny had forgotten all about that and had gone with her heart's desire. She blamed herself for turning a blind eye to the signs when Johnny controlled her movements, listened to her conversations on the phone, and did things like insist on taking and picking her from work. She had thought it was love and care.

There was no escape for her. Drugs and alcohol became an excuse for violence. Jenny believed the drugs and alcohol caused Johnny to be erratic and turned him into a monster – a monster that she couldn't tame.

Despite being battered, she had made excuses for him because he acted differently at times. However, in hindsight, she knew he had calculated all the barbaric acts. He fed her when he pleased. She sometimes went for days without food. She forgave him time and time again, hoping the torture would cease – to no avail. She had once thought he would change, and she had been willing to help him do that.

Although she had been blinded by him, she didn't want to shed tears for him. She felt it would have been a waste of her body fluid. Her forward-thinking had been captured and locked in, but she had the power of her mind and a voice.

Every time she tried to speak or twist the lock and release herself, she faced hostility, but she never gave up.

She knew that giving up was accepting defeat. She had the hope of escaping, but her strength was fading away rapidly.

Every time she tried to escape, when he gave her some freedom from the basement, he told her he was the only person who would put up with her ugly body and that no man would want her. He said to her that, if he couldn't have her, no other person would set his eyes on her because she belonged to him.

The words made Jenny believe it didn't matter where a man came from or whether or not a dowry was paid. Male dominance and control are the same everywhere. She was confident in her appearance, apart from the bruises he had caused her, so Johnny calling her ugly didn't make her see herself differently.

Jenny wondered how men could believe they own women as their property once they set their eyes and hands on them – how they can restrict their liberty and independence and make them their possessions.

When Johnny saw signs that she wanted to break free, he tightened the bolts of the doors, and the intimidation escalated. Johnny barred her from listening to any form of media. She had no family or friends to confide in, and she had no phone to contact her friends or the police. There were no neighbours to ask about her whereabouts.

She had no trouble fighting for what she wanted, but it seemed she was losing the battle. Jenny felt there was nothing she could do while locked in and guarded, but she was hopeful she would find a way to escape. She believed she was not destined to suffer forever.

CHAPTER 27

The Tormentor

Waiting  For

you....

Johnny's behaviour assured Jenny the monster was out of the closet. There was nowhere to hide. He had revealed who he was. She had no hope of him changing, and she wished she could be away from him. She felt she had learnt her lesson about not observing the signs of a disaster waiting to happen.

Their relationship had turned into a nightmare.

However, she couldn't show Johnny; she was scared. She wanted to prove to him that, although he could break her physically, inside she remained intact. Jenny was not ready to change who she was, as she was sure she had done nothing wrong. She considered Johnny to be the troubled one, for hitting a woman.

Her dream of gaining freedom from him became just a vision. Jenny regarded Johnny as a hurricane, ready to destroy every aspect of her life. He ruled by fear, and he stopped at nothing to get what he wanted. He used the words I love you regularly; in fact, he said it every time he hurt her and asked for forgiveness. Jenny wondered what love was supposed to mean in his mind because it had a different meaning to her.

With Jenny's continuous questioning and her refusal to respect and obey his authority, Johnny knew that his kingdom was about to fall apart. He knew his mission was fading, and he had to fight like a soldier to keep his presence felt. He felt that Jenny had turned out to be his enemy, and he was determined to conquer her.

His punches and kicks made her feel as if she was his rag doll. She remained determined to defeat the tyrant without using physical violence, but her emaciated body seemed to be giving up.

She was a lonely soul in what she had expected to be her castle– in a palace she had been determined to rule and control. She had never wanted to be lonely. Then again, reminiscing on her former life before Johnny, she knew she would have preferred to be alone rather than to be Johnny's punching bag. She wondered what had gone wrong and questioned herself about where their romance had disappeared to. She felt it would have been easier for her to blame herself, but she was pretty sure she was innocent.

Looking back at what her work colleague had said about Johnny, she realised she had been unable to trust the woman's warning because of her mistrust of the lady. She had believed her colleague had said what she'd spoken out of spite and jealousy of her picture-perfect life and that she wanted to cause trouble in her relationship.

Johnny's control of her social life was subtle and hadn't come across as controlling, to begin with – until she realised, she couldn't go anywhere without his permission. He monitored her movements through phone calls or by taking her wherever she wanted to go. Next came the threats. Jenny couldn't engage in a telephone conversation. Jhonny always asked who the caller was or stood close to Jenny to listen to the chat. And sometimes he would prevent her from taking a call altogether.

She had been afraid to walk away. Now, she knew she had to take a risk and break free. However, her plans had to be strategic and tactical because she had nowhere to run. It was as if Johnny's ghost was everywhere, watching and waiting to pounce on her. She faced his wrath and domination alone, locked away in the dark. She thought she was in a war zone, with an army attacking an innocent, harmless civilian.

Without her inner strength, she would have been dead. She had thought of going back to her country when the relationship had gone sour. But she hadn't known how to do that; Johnny had confiscated her passport, and she'd had no money.

He had made her a prisoner in the very place she'd envisioned turning into her palace.

Although her dignity had been stripped away, and her brain eroded by fear, she remained stable. She pondered about the past and how in love she and Johnny had been before her life had gone pear-shaped. But it was now just a dream. She was fearful that any move to demonstrate to Johnny how she felt inside would have spelt disaster. Her anxieties and terror made her remain in the position Johnny had set her in. Her legs felt like cooked spaghetti, but her determination kept her alive, and she refused to allow her self-worth to be broken.

However, while in the darkness, she was unable to see his punches landing on her face. To him, it seemed like a game. He would hit her, walk away, come back, and do it once more. He strangled her and told her he had her life in his hands and that he had the right to decide whether she lived or died. The basement was filled with her echoes of, "Please forgive me. I am sorry. I love you." She said these words knowing it was a way of seeking her survival. It was her only way to buy her liberty and to keep the peace.

She clutched onto her swelling stomach every time Johnny hit her to protect it from the blows that narrowly missed it. Jenny was sure she was not gaining weight. Over the past five years, during which she had been locked in the basement, she hardly ate enough to survive. But the fluttering in her stomach grew stronger by day.

A few months later, she felt and saw the outline of a tiny foot pushing against her belly. Jenny smiled and stroked her stomach when she learnt that something was growing inside her, but her joy was just as quickly overshadowed by her realisation of the kind of life she was leading. She hoped Johnny would have mercy for the sake of the unborn child.

She was fearful of adding a child to her turmoil. But on the other hand, she thought that Johnny would think about the baby and stop hurting her.

However, on one occasion, as the baby kicked in her stomach, Johnny stormed into the basement drunk, and her heart sunk. He smashed her face, and she collapsed onto the ground. Jenny felt the baby's kicks increase as she lay on the cold concrete as she prayed that nothing would happen to their child.

Johnny blamed her for his misfortunes and stormed back out of the cellar. Jenny felt lucky he hadn't kicked her in the stomach while she was down because his big boot would have met with their baby's tiny foot. But suddenly he reappeared and dragged her out of the cellar. She screamed at him, "Please don't hurt our baby!"

Like a flash, a blow landed on her stomach, and she fell to the floor with a thud. He dragged her back to the basement and pushed her to the ground.

He accused her of getting pregnant intentionally to trap him. Jenny did whatever she could to protect her growing bump from the blows. By doing so, she left her face exposed. Blood dripped from her face like red sweat while Johnny continued hitting her, accusing her of becoming pregnant on purpose to ruin his life. He dragged her by the leg and left her writhing in agony. Jenny clasped her bump with both hands "you will be okay. Mummy is here" she said.

Minutes later, she laid her hands on her stomach, and all was quiet. She felt no fluttering, not a single movement apart from the inflating and deflating of her tummy as she breathed in and out. Inside the cellar, everything was calm. Tears rolled down her cheeks as she wondered whether the baby was okay. She spoke to the baby, saying, "Everything will be all right." But suddenly, blood trickled down her legs, and tears flooded down her cheeks. She paced up and down, screaming at the top of her lungs, calling Johnny evil and a murderer. But the only thing she heard was the sound of her own voice.

She went to the door and pulled on the handle until her hands were raw, but the door wouldn't budge. As she screamed, she felt a tiny fluttering in her stomach. Her hands moved to her bump, and she felt her baby's foot. She looked around the four walls of the basement, but they were impenetrable. Not only was she trapped; the baby inside her was also in grave danger. She was determined to fight for its safety. However, she wondered how she could shelter the child when she couldn't protect herself.

She weighed up the present and the future, but she couldn't see a way forward. She was stagnant and stuck. Furthermore, her health was deteriorating. She couldn't get herself out of her present situation.

CHAPTER 28

The Pain of a Mother

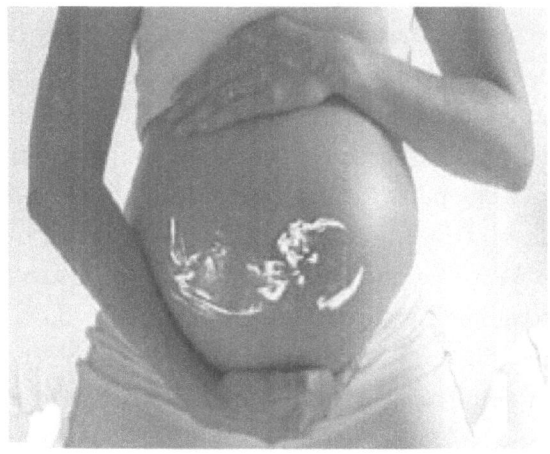

It's only a mother who knows the pain of a child.

Johnny didn't check on her until the following day, and he had no remorse for what he had done to her. His days out became longer, and he didn't care what time he arrived home. His absence intensified Jenny's fear because she didn't know what mood he would be in every time he came back.

She was left with an empty stomach. Johnny's excuse was that he had extra work to do at the office, or he had to wait for clients, and she wasn't allowed to question him. For some time, he seemed to have lost interest in her, and she went for days with no violence. She was happy that her body could rest from the blows. Only his shouts and her sobs were heard in the household as she begged him to save their unborn child.

Her bedroom eyes had turned into a well of tears as she reached the end of her tether. Jenny knewshe had to fight for her survival and that of the baby in her belly. She asked herself where the Johnny she had admired had gone. Instead of burning with desire, she shivered with terror when she heard the basement door open or when she smelt alcohol on his breath. The house had turned into a hub of horror instead of a house of laughter and happiness. She had to fulfil Johnny's demands, hoping that her womb would protect the baby inside her.

Many times, she felt suffocated under his massive weight, and her breathing became difficult. Johnny would get off her when her voice faded away, and she was at the brink of death. He tormented her by telling her not to worry because he was capable of giving her the 'kiss of life'.

To Jenny, Johnny was a dormant volcano. He was sometimes tender and calm one minute, and the next, a slight mistake would provoke him, and he would erupt and punch and kick her. He was in total control of her body. Jenny tried to fight back like a lioness trying to protect its cub from a predator, but her efforts were futile.

In her darkest moments, she lay on the cold concrete curled up like a ball of wool whispering to her unborn child to hang in there, but she couldn't overlook the fact that her days on earth were limited in Johnny's hands. She wondered about the fateful day that she'll have to give birth alone, locked in a basement with no medical assistance or comfort. She was only allowed to dress up for Johnny's eyes to admire.

She couldn't comprehend how her world had turned around. She felt dark clouds looming over her, and she couldn't take it anymore. One night, Jenny confronted Johnny. She told him she had about three more months left before she would give birth to their child, and there was no way she was going to deliver in the basement.

Johnny turned towards her and glared at her swelling stomach intensely with scornful eyes. Jenny listened to his heavy breathing. Without warning, he rushed towards her like lightening and punched her in the stomach. Jenny held her abdomen and leaned forward, screaming in agony. By the time Johnny stopped hitting her, her water had broken, and she was standing on a pool of her body fluid. She couldn't tell whether she had urinated on herself or whether she was about to give birth.

Jenny begged Johnny to take her to the hospital to save their child's life, even if hers didn't matter. But instead, he locked the basement door and left. He didn't come back until the following morning. Jenny gave birth to their premature twins – a boy and a girl – alone in the dark at night.

The babies died soon after birth, and Jenny was glued to the floor, covered in blood. She wailed continuously because of her children, who she named Liberty and Milo, they meant the world to her. But Johnny didn't seem to be bothered by what had happened. He asked Jenny to stand up, clean herself up, and make herself presentable.

Jenny stared at him and spat at him. From then on, her tears never dried. She believed the pain she had endured from him couldn't compare to the pain she felt over losing their children. She felt dead inside, but she refused to be broken.

Johnny tried to find a way to justify the suffering he caused her by blaming her for being strong-headed. He wanted to make sure Jenny shouldered the blame for his violence towards her, but she refused to take responsibility.

Realising that Jenny was never going to change, Johnny promised to let her out of the basement if she behaved herself. He asked her to promise never to confide in anybody about anything that had happened. If she did, he promised, she would die.

She accepted his demands, thinking she was finally going to get a chance to escape. However, she wasn't aware that Johnny would accompany her everywhere she went. He held her hand in public as if they were deeply in love and looked at her sternly and squeezed her hand every time someone spoke to her. She had no way of fleeing.

Johnny had a gun that he threatened to use on her if she attempted to run away. She was not allowed to use public toilets or leave his sight when they went out. She considered him a terrorist.

Before they went out, Johnny expected her to dress to his liking. But he soon complained she was spending too much time in front of the mirror. Moreover, she was putting on too much make-up. He accused her of wanting to attract attention from other men.

She stopped wearing make-up, but there was always something she wasn't doing right. Her style of dress became distasteful in Johnny's eyes. He forced her to watch him while he cut her clothes that he didn't like into pieces. He decided to choose what she wore whenever they ventured out.

When Johnny was busy, Jenny couldn't go out on her own without an escort, and she was given strict instructions not to defy the escort's orders.Jenny wasscared to confide in anybody about her nightmares in Johnny's hands. She thought a guard had been sent to spy on her. She was also afraid the escort had weapons. The man was stone-faced and watched her every move like a hawk.

Johnny had warned her to be ready for consequences if she went against his rules. When she was out, she always checked the time.

Jenny wasn't allowed to stay outlonger than the fixed period Johnny had allotted for her to spend out of the house.

Many times, she tried to sweet-talk her guard into letting her use the toilet, but he wouldn't even open his mouth or give her a smile. The bodyguard was tall, stocky, and mean-looking; he had a black moustache, long black hair in a ponytail and piercing green eyes. He communicated with Jenny through stern gestures. She thought that people might have thought she was a celebrity with her bodyguard. At times, she was tempted to shout and run for her life, but her instinct told her it was too dangerous.

Although Johnny still had a leash on her and controlled how far she could go, she considered herself lucky. She was able to breathe fresh air, she had some freedom, she had food, and Johnny treated her with chocolates and doughnuts. He wasn't hitting her, and it was only a matter of time before she found a way out.

She gained weight in the process, and the mental torment continued. Johnny referred to her like a pig and demanded she had to eat less. He weighed her food, and her weight dropped dramatically.

Johnny commented on skinny models that he saw in the media on how beautiful they looked, and she knew he was trying to mould her to the image he wanted.

Jenny knew the pictures in the media were altered to make the people appear flawless and attract the viewers; she believed that no woman was as perfect as those in the media and magazines and no woman would defeat her in competition for natural beauty. Jenny thought she didn't need to lose weight or wear make-up to look beautiful.

Jenny never admired the pictures in the media. She loved her curves, but Johnny dictated what she had to do. Protecting herself by whatever means was her priority. But at size six, she looked at herself in the mirror and saw a reflection of a large woman staring back at her. It was how Johnny described her. Being called fat and ugly even after losing weight meant she was fighting a losing battle. Something sparked inside her, and she felt she was never going to be good enough in his eyes.

Her body fought back because of lack of enough nutrients to survive. Johnny had cut out the doughnuts, chocolates and he only fed her when he wished. She was on the verge of physical collapse. Jenny had to choose between Johnny's demands or her health, but she had no choice. She battled the two giants' singlehandedly. Her weight loss didn't change Johnny's attitude towards her. He called her names, and the thinner she became the more Johnny taunted her.

Her breasts became flattened, and Johnny told her she had to have breast implants to make him happy. Jenny felt she had no strength to fight him. Johnny decided on the breast implants Jenny was going to have and demanded to be with her during the surgery. The procedure caused complications later, and the implants were removed. Johnny blamed her for wasting his money on the operation. But the process wasn't her choice.

Jenny hoped to break free one day and stop trembling every time she heard Johnny's footsteps. When the door banged open, she felt like a bullet was piercing her heart. A small blunder saw her fly in the air from his kicks. She was always in front of the firing squad. Jenny was surprised that she was still alive. Peace was something she had forgotten about. But it was close, yet so far away.

With time, she felt enough was enough. She knew that by staying and doing nothing, she was ensuring she would face more years of tribulations. She had to save herself, as she had run out of ideas to please Johnny.

She gathered the strength she had left, both physical and mental, and convinced herself she still had power left inside her and it had to come out. It was the only way she felt she could attain her liberty and set herself free from Johnny's shackles.

However, her signs of wanting to break free escalated the matter. Arguments turned to blows. She became a workout machine, where Johnny did his muscle-building exercises. He suppressed her power, but she kept on fighting. He knew she had no physical strength, but he couldn't underestimate her interior dominance.

Jenny always had a perfect excuse for her injuries when strangers commented on her bruises on the streets. She told them she banged herself on the doorframe or tripped over something. Those were her perfect excuses, as she went everywhere with Johnny. The house stopped being a fierce torture chamber, except for the occasional slaps, punches and a kick every now and again. Yet again, just when she thought things were getting better, things fell apart.

She couldn't pretend any longer. She could see Johnny was afraid of losing her, and that was why he kept her on a leash. When he realised, he was about to lose his control, he changed his tactics and camouflaged like a soldier on the battlefield.

He realised he was sleeping with an enemy that could strike at any time because Jenny never surrendered to him. Jenny, on the other hand, felt she was living with an animal that couldn't be tamed. Jenny thought if she had taken time to read Johnny, she could have guarded her herself. She wished for the day the anguish would finally be over.

CHAPTER 29

The Heartbreaker

An exposed heart is open to abuse.

Jenny regretted the day she met Johnny. She compared his love to a chemical reaction that reacted in her heart, making it easy for him to penetrate it. She had surrendered her love to him and had given him everything he wanted without limit, ignoring her intuitions even when she knew what was happening to her was not right.

The fearless princess had been reduced to jelly – to a defenceless human being. She had been consumed by her desire to be Johnny's queen and had wanted their love to last forever, but things had turned sour. It wasn't how she wanted it to end.

The love they had once shared was nothing she had experienced before, and she couldn't resist it. But when she thought about it now, she saw that it was all a lie. The signs had been visible, but she had turned a blind eye. She'd felt blown away by his love and attention. She had done everything he'd asked her to. However, everything Johnny had told Jenny was calculated – a way to hook her, like a fish in the deep blue sea. He had cast the bait, and she had been caught and unable to wriggle herself free.

He had no love for her. Jenny couldn't believe she hadn't seen her suffering coming. The passion had been so sweet and vigorous. Johnny could do nothing wrong in her eyes. Everything about him was just perfect. He was the man of her dreams – a knight in shining armour. She couldn't believe what was happening. It seemed like she was in the light one minute, and all of a sudden, darkness had engulfed her world like a total solar eclipse.

Piece by piece, her heart had been ripped into chunks, and her world had fallen apart. She had sunk deeper into Johnny's world of violence. She had tried hard to keep afloat, but Johnny had pushed her further and further, moving her steadily to where he wanted her to be. Jenny never imagined that 'everlasting love' would come crashing in on her and leave her in a daze. Jenny never believed she'd weep until her tears streamed like a river, eventually leaving her with no more tears to cry. She became numb to the mistreatment, and her hopes and dreams were shattered. But she didn't believe it was over yet.

Jenny felt like a broken mirror. She knew that, even if she had a chance to fix herself, the cracks would be visible for the rest of her life, and the inner torment would live with her forever. However, her hopes and vision were what kept her alive, and she knew she couldn't let her past rule her future.

She yearned for peace in her heart. She had never imagined that Johnny could do what he had done to her. Love to her was a fairy tale. It was in the centre of her heart, and she felt saturated by it. But for Johnny, love didn't mean a thing.

Jenny's tears were like a hidden stream. No one knew or could imagine the ache in her heart. She had perfected a way of hiding her real emotion. Her heartbeat raised during explosive episodes, and she avoided closing her eyes. She was afraid she might never open them again.

She had nowhere to hide. Jenny blamed herself for letting Johnny play her like a puppet on a string. They had two different lives, but she had believed they were joined as one. Soon, though, Jenny had realised it was just a dream. She acknowledged that too much of anything was poisonous. His eyes told one story while his heart said another.

Jenny couldn't read his heart, and his eyes fooled her and took her to cloud nine. But when she found herself back on earth, she had to protect her heart and planned to sneak out of the darkness. It made her realise she had woken up from the nightmare and had come back to reality.

Jenny's aspirations in life before she'd embarked on her journey to freedom gave her the courage to fight on for her liberty. She reminded herself she was still active in mind and soul and vowed never to let Johnny take her freedom away again. She saw his reflection staring back at her, but she refused to play the victim game. She listed the assets she would rely on to free herself:

- Eyes to focus on her next move
- Brains to figure out how to tackle things and plan her exit
- Ears to listen to what was best for her
- Hands she would lay on positive things
- A figure to walk majestically with her head held high
- A nose to smell a rat and avoid the traps
- The power to destroy early advances of destruction
- And legs to make that first step to freedom, empowerment, and success.

CHAPTER 30

Breaking Free

The joy of freedom

Jenny thought of how many times she had the power to flee her abusive relationship but had found it difficult to leave, thinking that Johnny was going to change. She had lived in fear and lost her dignity and her children in the process, but she had not lost her self-worth. Jenny felt her courage and the strength to defend herself was intact. But how could she compete with Johnny when she had no way out?

She knew Johnny thought he had brainwashed her to believe that she had lost all the control and that he was the only person who held her life. She was afraid that leaving without a plan would put her life in danger and that no man who held power and control would give it up lightly without a fight.

Jenny understood that contemplating leaving was a huge risk. Therefore, she had to make a careful and strategic plan. However, Jenny had no means of communication with anyone, and Johnny kept the house keys with him. She vowed the next time they went out she would do whatever it took to escape.

Her journey to freedom had been out of the question while she remained locked up, but that period hadn't been her end either. During it, daylight had been a thing of the past. The closed basement door had isolated her from the outside world. She had only seen the light when Johnny felt like allowing her to view it. She knew what she needed was to find a small space through which to squeeze herself – a hidden exit that would take her outside the house and allow her to break out to freedom. But the walls around her were sealed tightly with bricks and cement.

Johnny made sure the openings around the house were secured continuously, and he was confident no one was looking for her. Therefore, her liberation depended on him. She followed his rules, thinking he would be lenient. She had faith that one day, the prison door would open, and she would fly back to freedom. She aimed to plan her mission with top secrecy and bring an end to her lengthy confinement.

Jenny felt like a mole trying to break the earth and lift its head from below the ground. However, Johnny's thick boots kept her below the surface, but she was determined to break free. Jenny pretended nothing was wrong in hopes that Johnny would lessen his grip on her. She was aware he was afraid of losing control and believed revenge was the only way to regain his reign.

For Jenny, her idle mind enabled her to reflect on her life. She saw that crying was pointless when there was no one to wipe her tears. She ran through her options and pondered how it would feel to be liberated again, and the thought of it made her stronger. She believed she could resist his chain and have her voice heard since Johnny had loosened his grip on her in the house. But this was not to be.

One evening, Johnny burst into the house through the kitchen door and saw a phone fly from Jenny's hand. He had left his mobile phone as a trap. As quick as lightning, he shot forward straight to her and shouted, "Woman, you are mine. If you ever leave, that will be the end. Do you hear me!?"

Jenny jumped. She trembled like an earthquake when Johnny told her that calling the cops won't help her. Just when Jenny thought the opportunity to run had availed itself, the real Johnny had returned. She had been threatened many times, so she knew Johnny was looking for a fight. He slurred his words, and Jenny didn't open her mouth. She didn't want to fuel the fire by replying to him, but the lack of response made him wild with anger. He snarled at the fact she was ignoring him and told her she thought of herself as very smart.

He told her any attempt to leave would force him to carve her body with his bare hands and shape her in a way that would ensure that no other man would ever set his eyes on her. He seemed like a storm, and Jenny moved away from him to a corner of the room.

He warned her that, if she ever ignored him or betrayed him, she should consider herself dead. And no one would care because he was her master. He said to her if she wanted to live longer, she should respond to his command, never interfere with his stuff, and never question his authority. Only then, when she avoids igniting his anger would she have peace. Jenny knew what happened when Johnny spoke in a particular way. He told her she was better off in her dungeon if she disobeyed him because that was where she belonged.

With those words, she knew her days of setting herself free were limited and that her fate was in Johnny's hands. It was the one opportunity Jenny had to escape. She pleaded with him not to send her back into the basement. Johnny listened and ordered her to prepare supper for him. But as soon as she opened the fridge door, he stormed into the kitchen and kicked the fridge door.

Jenny fell to his feet and declared her love for him, as doing so seemed like a good idea. It was the only tactic she had up her sleeve,

the only way she had to change his mind and secure her release. She was ready to do anything to ensure her peace.

Instead, Johnny responded with a kick, and she flew, slamming into the fridge with a bang. Things that had been sitting on the refrigerator clattered to the ground around her as she supported herself. He swept everything from the countertop with his hand, sending utensils, bowls and appliances flying in different directions, many of them hitting her body. Jenny said a little prayer and curled up under the rubble, but she had no more tears to cry.

She let him kick her without a fight because shouting fuelled his anger. She groaned and moaned, but in the back of her mind, she calculated her plans to flee if she remained alive. The only thing that stopped her was lack of a safe passage and keys to open the doors.

To Jenny's surprise, Johnny removed the keys from his pockets and held them in his hand. As she avoided staring at him, she hoped he would put the keys down and forget about them. Jenny was still lying on the kitchen floor soaked in blood, and she didn't know for how long she had been lying there. Johnny left the kitchen and walked towards the living room without a word looking as if he had come from a slaughterhouse.

Jenny laid quietly, in the kitchen, waiting until she heard Johnny'sloud snore. Her first thought was it was an excellent chance to break free as Johnny slept, but she had no keys. Jenny examined herself and noticed her broken finger. She was sure he had broken her ribs, as she'd heard a crack when he had kicked her. She scanned around her and saw a chunk of her hair. Her head felt like it had been stung by bees, and blood oozed from every part of her body. Johnny had left her for dead, but she convinced herself it was time to break the chains; it was now or never.

Within a short while, Johnny's snoring filled the house, and that confirmed to Jenny he was in a dreamland. However, she was afraid to do anything in case it was a trap. She was sure it was her final day, and she had to make her last attempt to run off. She crawled to the living room, knowing very well she was approaching the danger zone.

"This is the moment to break the chains and find my freedom, she told herself."

Though Johnny was fast asleep, Jenny shook like a leaf. She knew even a small mistake would mean pushing her to death. Jenny gathered her strength and staggered to her feet. Her heart pounded, and she was sure Johnny would hear it beating.

Slowly, she staggered to the living room at a snail's pace and saw the keys on the coffee table. Very gently, Jenny walked to the table and grasped the keys in her hand. As she moved her hand to her chest, a surge of energy filled her body. Every step she made brought her closer to the free world.

As she dragged herself to the door, she looked back and saw a trail of her blood following her and Johnny sprawled out on the grey leather settee snoring. Within seconds, the snoring stopped. She froze on the spot like a statue, holding her breath. She glared at Johnny and then glanced towards the door. She decided bolting was too risky.

Then suddenly, Johnny turned to one side, facing away from the door, and Jenny's heart came alive again.

Slowly and very carefully, she reached for the door handle and opened the door. Suddenly, she felt the cold breeze brush her bloody face as she smelt the scent of freedom. Her heart beat like crazy, and a chill ran through her body. She doubted whether she could outrun Johnny if he caught her escaping. But as soon as she took the first step out of the door, Jenny felt like she was entering into a new world – the world where she belonged. Adrenaline pumped through her veins. Her freedom was so near, yet so far away. She shivered uncontrollably, knowing that, if Johnny woke up and found her fleeing, he would run after her and finish her off.

Jenny's stomach turned to ice when she thought of Johnny's death-like eyes, devoid of all emotions staring at her.She wondered whether her emancipation from slavery and Johnny's iron hands was going to last. Through the darkness, she saw a glimpse of light on the horizon and ran as fast as she could, and despite her pace slowing down; she felt as if her legs run like a cheetah. She forgot about all the aches and pain and increased her speed with every step she made.

It was her moment to run, just like she had done when she was young. Jenny reminded herself that it was not her mistake that had kept her locked up; it was Johnny's insecurity that had driven him to deprive her of her independence. In all of what had happened, Jenny felt she was the strong one mentally.

As she increased her pace with much effort, she saw a figure in the distance. She shouted in a fading voice, "Help, help!" Her chest felt like it was collapsing, but she couldn't stop running.

The person on the horizon stopped and looked back but paid little attention to her.

Jenny shouted again, "Help!"

The person stopped and walked towards her cautiously. She begged the stranger to help her. The man asked her what had happened, but she was out of breath and could only mumble some words. As the man called for an ambulance, she collapsed to the ground.

When she opened her eyes, she found herself lying on a hospital bed with monitors on her body. She also had a cast on her right hand,and for a moment, she had no idea where she was until she set her eyes on the doctors who surrounded her. She thought it was a dream until someone spoke to her and asked her how she was feeling.

She was informed she had been in a coma for two weeks and considered herself lucky to be alive. She immediately thought she wouldn't be out of the woods until Johnny had been arrested. She knew her escape was going to open a new chapter in her life.

While she was at the hospital, Jenny thought about how women presenting their cases to the authorities are disregarded, often due to lack of evidence and often until it is too late. She worried she would be forced to go back to Johnny if he insisted on taking her home because that is what happens in her community.

The thought of being around Johnny made her shudder. She didn't recognise her reflection when she looked at herself in the mirror. Her skin was covered with bruises.

Although the doctors had tried to fix her body, she knew that her beauty lay beneath her skin.

When Jenny felt better, she was asked to write a statement of what had happened.

Upon seeing Jenny on the news, Johnny had gone to the police and told them Jenny was attacked during a night out. However, her version of the story was different. She was asked whether she wanted to go back home or to a safe place, and the thought of setting her eyes on Johnny made her stomach churn.

Jenny later hobbled into a vehicle and told she was going to a refuge for women. While at the shelter, she met women who had escaped domestic violence.

Looking at them and listening to their stories made Jenny understand that there are a lot of women around the world who suffer barbaric treatment in men's hands for years. And not all of them have physical scars, but the wounds they harbour within are immense, and their hearts bleed with pain. Some might not have been locked up in their houses, but the fear instilled in them kept them prisoners of their partners' authority.

The women had been forced to remain in the relationships.And had learned to live with the savagery until they gathered the courage to make a bold move after suffering for years. But some never make it.

Jenny observed that, despite being in a safe environment, some of the women had nightmares every day. This demonstrated the hold the men had on them, even in their absence. They believed their partners could get hold of them and take them back into their homes. Jenny observed that the women had been made to think they could run, but they couldn't hide, just as Johnny had made her believe.

She told the women she met at the safe housethat it was true that they couldn't hide, but where there is an opportunity to escape, they should resist manipulation. She told them that with their courage, willpower, and support, they were capable of changing their lives. Fear and self-doubt, she explained, is women's most significant enemy that leave them exposed to their men's insecurities.

She appreciated the support from the staff at the women's shelter, which did everything they could to support the women and help them rebuild their self-esteem, which had been shattered by the emotional abuse they had endured. They had been made to feel unattractive without caking themselves with make-up, valueless in society, and unworthy, despite some of them being professionals and looking stunning in their natural beauty.

Jenny heard that while she was in the hospital, the police had no information about her. Her work colleagues had spotted her case in the media and alerted Johnny. He had warned them not to say a thing to the police.

However, the police learnt from Stephanie that the last time Jenny's workmates had heard from her, she had told them she was back in Kenya. Her best friend, Stephanie, had remained suspicious and had reported the matter to the police. But no progress was made on the case.

Therefore, her colleagues were surprised to learn that she had never actually left for Kenya. They'd wondered why she had gone without saying goodbye and without even informing them of her departure until they'd gotten a call from her to say she was in Kenya. Even then, she hadn't said much.

Jenny didn't know what her future held, but she was happy she was free at last. Johnny was arrested, and the police recovered videos that helped them with their investigation in Johnny's case. When Jenny was comfortable to talk, she narrated her story to the police. Jenny told the cops all she wanted since coming to the country was to have a happy marriage, and she was determined to work to get to the top of her career. Instead, she had become Johnny's prisoner because she refused to be controlled.

The police officers asked Jenny if she knew that Johnny was a human trafficker and whether she had seen women in the house or on any other premises. It made sense to Jenny about the girls who had come to the house. The police unearthed Johnny's secrets and discovered he was a human trafficker, part of a cartel, and arrested some of his human trafficking accomplices.

Johnny had no idea how Jenny managed to escape because he had left her for dead. He always kept the house keys in his pocket. He couldn't understand why he had fallen asleep and left the keys on the table.

Jenny, on the other hand, knew that Johnny was never going to be subjected to similar ordeal to the one he had exposed her to in the dungeon. But at least his liberty had been taken away, just as he had taken hers. His money couldn't buy his freedom. His smugness flattened like a pierced balloon. Jenny finally received the justice she deserved. Johnny received a life sentence for attempted murder, forced confinement, and human trafficking.

CHAPTER 31

Self-Healing

When you fall, don't give up, take baby steps, spread your wings, and fly again.

After Johnny's sentencing, Jenny pondered the notion that tens of thousands of women go through situations that are similar to the one she'd endured – with no voice and no hope of ever saving themselves or being rescued.

While others languish behind closed doors, disempoweredand brainwashed, and they receive no justice from the authorities.

No one cares about them. The women are held captive not only by self-doubt but also by fear, spouses, families, their communities, the lawmakers and society at large.

They are unable to break free from the bondage, and when they do, they are manipulated, and at timescaptured, and headed back to their tormentors. Therefore, the cycle of abuse continues.

The professionals and the communities that are supposed to help and support the females blame the women for staying in volatile relationships and also blame them for leaving. The peoplein power don't understand how it feels for the women to live in fear of the unknown. Not unless they have been in their shoes. On the other hand, society sits back as a spectator as the women suffer, doing nothing to put an end to their misery.

Jenny recognised that the lack oftaking action by the authority against the perpetrators reinforces the offenders' power and control. It encourages the culprits to feel untouchable and push them to commit a worse crime.

By visualising her experience, Jenny felt victims are afraid to contemplate their escape, and some meet their untimely deaths for bringing shame to their spouses, families or for trying to run away. It is the ultimate price they pay for defying the rules and for spreading their wings in a world that is dominated by men's power.

Jenny strived to gain freedom in her motherland and ran away from home to escape the family's customs and tradition of oppression, forced marriage, and denial of education. She didn't know that she would be faced with new sets of problems in a foreign land. She acknowledged her trials and war weren't over yet, as she remained surrounded by men and women who do nothing to protect those who are downtrodden.

Jenny realised that everywhere she went, she would face male dominance. But her strength, empowerment, courage, and education were the weapons she held dear; with them, she would fight for her self-determination.

Nonetheless, she knew they wouldn't be enough without help from the men and women in the society who could and should be women's allies through actions against the structures that allow for widespread abuse of women.

She concluded that she could make a difference to women's freedom. But a massive long-term impact is only possible if women collaborate and speak the same language for their redemption. She needed the women to unite and become UNITED WOMEN OF THE WORLD and fight the battle against being seen as inferior – the struggle to be recognised, respected, treated like human beings and to be given equal opportunities as men in salaries, job opportunities, in matters concerning nation-building and in every public and private sector.

Jenny had a vision that, one day, men will have respect for women and recognise females are not born to suffer but to enjoy life just like men do and to rule the world.

Jenny vowed never to be controlled by a man again. She had fallen into Johnny's love trap, and it was a lesson she'd learnt the hard way. Johnny had come into her life as a guardian wearing armour. Before long, she found herself unable to resist him. She had gotten lost in his world and had been laid bare by his lust for dominance. Her world had become a distant memory, but she had high hopes to rise up again.

After her turbulent time with Johnny, Jenny was ready to rebuild her life once she healed the external physical scars. She knew the internal psychological wounds would live with her forever. However, Jenny wasn't willing to settle for defeat, even though she couldn't erase the past. Moreover, she couldn't let the past define her as a woman or define her next course.

When the coast was clear, and the tides had calmed down, Jenny realised that money can never buy love and fairy tales are just a dream. They don't exist, and no one knows what is inside a person's mind, what someone else is about, or what happens behind closed doors. Only the perpetrators, the victims, and the four walls of a house know the truth. But the walls are silent witnesses.

Jenny went through the process of self-healing through the help of her friend Stephanie and counselling. She tried to stop the flashback of her experience, but they continued to haunt her. No therapy could stop her from feeling hurt. However, she knew that she was her biggest healer and refused to let her inner feelings prevent her from being the person she wanted to be. She learnt a lesson – that not everything that glittered was gold.

She woke up from the nightmare and walked tall. Though she found herself in the desert, she had to breathe the fresh air and let the oxygen oxygenate her system and get rid of Johnny's carbon dioxide before it poisoned her forever.

The toxic relationship almost killed her. She had tried to make Johnny see she was her own person. She was free and stronger at last. Jenny couldn't let his memory ruin her future. She had to spread her wings like an eagle and fly again.

It was time for a fresh start, but she knew it was never going to be a comfortable journey. Her determination and support played a significant role in her self-rediscovery.

She remembered the warrior princess before Johnny had crawled into her life and lured her into letting her guard down and welcomed him into her life. She felt like the queen of the castle was back with a vengeance, when Johnny had believed he'd faded all the colours in her skin and broken her down. She imagined his reflection staring back at her, but she promised herself it could never hurt her.

Jenny felt there was no need to cry for the time lost.

She had to let go of the toxic past and focus on the future. She determined to break the chains of Johnny's dominance in every way. She viewed her experience as a bad nightmare. Closing the door and harbouring herself in the house wasn't something that entered her mind; life had to go on. To her, the sea was full of fish, but she had to take the time to explore it to avoid attracting the sharks.

CHAPTER 32

The Nightmare Returns

Finally, he was where he belonged.

Just when Jenny was trying to rebuild her life, Johnny decided to crawl back, reaching out from behind prison bars with an apology letter for treating her like a caged animal. He thought that she was going to forgive him the way she had always forgiven him. Johnny declared his love for Jenny. He told Jenny lockingher up was to demonstrate the love in his heart for her.Andthat his care and love was forever. He said he was scared to lose her to another man, and that was why he was protective.

Jenny refused to fall for his tricks and considered him sick in the head to think she would crawl back to him. She had saved herself from the mouth of the lion, and there was no way she would dream of falling back into his arms. Thinking about it left a bad taste in her mouth. The thought of it made her shiver, and she wasn't afraid to tell him so.

Jenny refused to have Johnny control her life from behind bars. However, she knew he was a man with many connections and that he was dangerous. She believed that, if he were released from prison, he would go searching for her. He reminded her there was nothing that could separate them.

Johnny's obsession with Jenny and the thought of losing his control over her made him determined to fight back while in jail – to regain his power over her at all cost. He warned Jenny that, if she thought about going out with someone else, she would put her life and that person's life in danger. Therefore, the best thing to do was for her to wait for him so that they could start life afresh.

Jenny was aware these were not empty threats. Johnny was capable of doing anything. But he had no hold of her.

She wasn't in the dungeon where he had kept her invisible to the outside world. She told him she couldn't hold her breath any longer. She was untouchable, and she was going to play by her rules.

She relocated to a different town and started a new life. When she pondered on how her life had been before Johnny had taken control, she knew life would be hard. However, giving up on her journey to a life that she had set out to achieve wasn't something that crossed her mind. Johnny didn't get the best of her. She had her inner power intact, she was not over yet, and nothing was going to hold her down.

She felt she had to stand up and speak, and there was nothing but her way. Johnny was out of her life. To get closure, she wanted to say to him the words that she had struggled to get out of her mouth. Jenny wasn't afraid of Johnny andwas no longer his slave or property anymore. He had no power over her; he couldn't stop her from doing what she wished.

Jennyfelt that she was ready to face Johnny in prison and voice her inner feelings to him in person once and for all as she slipped on her black stiletto, black trouser suit and fixed the collar of her white blouse and grabbed her designer handbag. She'd had no time to speak to him before, but she was clear on what she wanted to say to him.

As Jenny walked with her head held up high through the prison gates, she knew it was time – time to put Johnny in his place. She stated her details at the reception, had her handbag checked, signed her name, and her body was scannedbefore she was led to the visiting area. As shecast her eyes around the prison walls, Jenny wished she was in charge so that she could make Johnny pay for every day he had held her captive.

Jenny didn't want to have any physical contact with Johnny. Therefore, she asked to speak to him from behind the glass in prison. "This is it," she said to herself.

She walked through the corridor to the visiting area. Soon her eyes caught up with Johnny's as he strolled towards her with a big smile, looking powerless in his prison uniform. She gave him a humourless grin and asked, "How does it feel to be locked up? Nice, eh?"

Johnny glared at her without a word. Jenny didn't want to say much to him. She looked him in the eye and said, "It's over. Goodbye, my love. I am in control of my destiny. My life is my choice. May you rot in hell!" Saying those words to Johnny lit a light in her heart, and she felt ten feet tall.

She felt liberated, and she had her power back. Johnny thought he had broken her, but nobody, not a single person, could capture her inner strength.Although he'd left her with cracks, he couldn't tear her internaldrive. Jenny told Johnny her heart didn't belong to him and never going to steal it again. Moreover, she had given him what he wanted, and they could have had it all. But it was never enough. Jenny told him she should have known sooner what she was getting herself into. She had thought what they'd shared was true love, but it had all been a lie. With those words, she walked straight to the door with her head held up high and a swagger in her steps, and she didn't look back.

She smiled and swayed her hips as she strode back to her freedom while she left Johnny locked up. She thought love may have led to her powers being taken away, but she vowed never to let her colours be eroded by anyone. Her promise to herself was never to allow another human being to dictate her destiny.

She had the strength of a woman. It was not in the form of muscles, but she had an inner power that Johnny couldn't take away.

She hoped that every woman could find her inner might and use it to her advantage. She wanted all women to realise they are their own bosses and to love who they are and never change for a man unless he did the same for them without coercion.

Jenny experienced flashbacks of her torment and, it was a bitter lesson for her to forget. She was left with the image of the man whom she had loved and who had brutalised her. It was not a mistake that the picture was ingrained in her memory. She wanted to delete the recollection of her ordeal and Johnny's image from her memory permanently. She hit the delete button in her mind, but the recycle bin wouldn't empty its contents, but nothing was ever going to hold her back.

Jenny, at first thought the world is sick. But she quickly realised it isn't the hostile world but the people in it. She had to move on and lead her life, but she knew she would carry a piece of Johnny with her forever. Regrets are the fuel of a torturous past. Therefore, for her, there was no looking back.

However, she had to draw from her past to enhance her feminine strength and move on.

Jenny felt her life was like thousands of jigsaw puzzles that had been spread far and wide, and she had to pick up the pieces one at a time and put them back together again. She knew the task was going to take time, and the result would be sweet. The thought enabled her to gain her vigour. She decided, after all, she was still Jenny, the warrior princess. She didn't need to change a thing about herself.

She wasn't the one with a problem, and she was not ready to let her dream fly away. She had to chase it.

She had ventured into her dreamland to conquer the world, and she had to continue with her fight and not let her existence to be dominated by a single direction. Moreover, her experience hadn't killed her; it had made her stronger.

After visiting the prison, Jenny went back to the house of horror. She collected the bracelet and the necklace her mother had given to her. They were safely placed in a box and hidden away. She put them on and suddenly, she felt a surge of intense force run through her body like an electric shock, and she knew it was time to emancipate girls and women from mental and societal slavery fully informed of their diversity and there was nothing that would stand in her way or stop her from fulfilling her desire. But will the women sing her song without fear, or will they turn their backs on her?

THE ROOT OF WOMEN'S DIFFICULTIES

We All Need to Act

Many elements contribute to women's misery, and every case is unique. But fear, lack of self-confidence, self- doubt, poverty, cultural practices, customs, traditions, beliefs, lack of education and leaving oneself exposed to manipulation are factors that play a significant role in setting women up to fail. Also, domination and control by men, lack of equal opportunities, oppression, discrimination, and violence are societal giants that hold women by the neck and suffocate them, shutting down their voices.

Change is the key for both men and women. Women should take actions to ensure they are afforded their rights, and men should reflect on their deeds and break the cycle of violence against women. Saving the young generation is crucial for we are their role models for a better future. It is time to revolutionise the way men and women think and act towards each other to make a difference in their situations.

If women and men don't speak the same language of changing the cultural beliefs against girls and women, nothing will ever change regarding violence against girls and women. The world will sit back and watch while men with evil intentions destroy the next generation of young girls and women for their own pleasure.

United women of the world unite!
Freedom is never voluntarily given by the oppressor; it must be demanded by the
oppressed.
—Martin Luther King, Jr.

ACKNOWLEDGEMENTS

I thank my children, Caitlin and Gregory, for their patience while I wrote the book and their support and prayers.

I give gratitude to God for his grace and for giving me the courage and concentration to pursue the writing of the book while I was going through the toughest time in my life. During this time, I was also pursuing a social work degree.

Writing this book acted as a stress relief strategy and allowed me to focus my mind on something different.

Also, I attribute the photos of the bench, the cave and the waterfall to 'jambonairobi.co.ke.'

BIOGRAPHY

MG Wanjiku was born in Kenya and lives in Derby in the United Kingdom. She is a mother of two sons and a daughter.

Her work consists of working in the social sector with deprived families in Kenya, children with special needs in the school environment in both Kenya and the United Kingdom, and secondary school students in the UK as a supply teacher. She also worked with the elderly in social care and clients with substance misuse issues in the UK and volunteered with various children's services and served as a board member and supported parents as a representative on the board.

She recently graduated with a BA (Hons) Social Work degree. The empowerment of women and ensuring women's rights matter in society remain her greatest passions.

BLURB

Jenny's destiny was determined at birth. Her future husband was ready and waiting to take her for a wife soon after she was born.

However, she refused to abide by the tribal customs. Her desire to build queendom to rule and control and to fight for women's liberation set her on a different course.

But when she locked eyes with Johnny, a millionaire mogul who travelled to Kenya from England in search of his kingdom and a place of tranquillity, life was never the same again.

At first, they tried to show each other up, seemingly vying for dominance. But he was ready to be the gentleman. Or was he?

When they left for England, Jenny never anticipated what would transpire in the process of her quest for independence. However, she was not ready to give up. Freedom was in her DNA, but what seemed to be the truth wasn't as she had thought...

www.ingramcontent.com/pod-product-compliance
Lightning Source LLC
Chambersburg PA
CBHW061620100726
47898CB00002B/751